I0537165

FEATHERS LEFT AROUND

FLEMING STONE MYSTERIES

The Clue (1909)
The Gold Bag (1910).
A Chain of Evidence (1912)
The Maxwell Mystery (1913)
Anybody But Anne (1914)
The White Alley (1915)
The Curved Blades (1915)
The Mark of Cain (1917)
Vicky Van (1918)
The Diamond Pin (1919)
Raspberry Jam (1920)
*The Mystery of the
   Sycamore* (1921)
The Mystery Girl (1922)
Feathers Left Around (1923)
Spooky Hollow (1923)
The Furthest Fury (1924)
Prillilgirl (1924)
Anything But the Truth (1925)
*The Daughter of the
   House* (1925)
The Bronze Hand (1926)
The Red-Haired Girl (1926)
The Vanity Case (1926)
All at Sea (1927)
Where's Emily (1927)
The Crime in the Crypt (1928)
The Tannahill Tangle (1928)
*The Tapestry Room
   Murder* (1928)
Triple Murder (1929)
The Doomed Five (1930)
The Ghosts' High Noon (1930)
Horror House (1931)
The Umbrella Murder (1931)

Fuller's Earth (1932)
*The Roll-Top Desk
   Mystery* (1932)
The Broken O (1933) (also
   published as *Honeymoon
   Murder*)
The Clue of the Eyelash (1933)
The Master Murderer (1933)
Eyes in the Wall (1934)
The Visiting Villain (1934)
The Beautiful Derelict (1935)
For Goodness' Sake (1935)
The Wooden Indian (1935)
The Huddle (1936)
In the Tiger's Cage (1936)
Money Musk (1936)
Murder in the Bookshop (1936)
The Mystery of the Tarn (1937)
The Radio Studio Murder (1937)
Gilt Edged Guilt (1938)
The Killer (1938)
The Missing Link (1938)
Calling All Suspects (1939)
Crime Tears On (1939)
*The Importance of Being
   Murdered* (1939)
Crime Incarnate (1940)
Devil's Work (1940)
Murder On Parade (1940)
Murder Plus (1940)
The Black Night Murders (1941)
Murder at the Casino (1941)
Murder Will In (1942)
Who Killed Caldwell? (1942)

FEATHERS
LEFT AROUND

CAROLYN WELLS

wildsidepress.com

WILDSIDE PRESS

Originally published in 1922, 1923.
Published by Wildside Press, LLC.
Visit us online at wildsidepress.com.

INTRODUCTION,
BY KARL WURF

Carolyn Wells (1862–1946) embarked on a prolific literary career that spanned various genres before cementing her legacy in mystery. Initially recognized for her whimsical verse, children's literature, and intricate puzzles, Wells discovered the burgeoning detective fiction genre and, around 1909, made a pivotal shift to writing mysteries. Her immense popularity and prolific output in the United States led many to call her "the American Agatha Christie," highlighting her status as a leading figure in the genre's Golden Age.

Wells's influence on the American mystery genre is undeniable. She contributed significantly to popularizing the puzzle plot mystery, setting a precedent for intricate narratives driven by intellectual challenges and clever deceptions. Her enduring

The Fleming Stone series, featuring the urbane and intellectual amateur detective, became her most celebrated work, encompassing over sixty novels. These stories often presented readers with complex scenarios, baffling disappearances, and cunningly devised crimes, cementing Wells's reputation as a master of the classical detective novel.

CHAPTER 1

LITTLE ANNA

KNOX flung his book across the veranda.

"Another of those old Sealed Room plots," he complained, as his host, Valentine Loft looked up, mildly inquiring.

"Man dead in an inaccessible room," Knox went on, "doors and windows all locked, no weapon to be found; murder or suicide?—and how was it done—if any?"

"The sort I like best," and Loft looked interested. "I eat up Detective Stories, and I like better the How Was It Done? or the Who Did It? kind better than the Why?"

"You're dead wrong. The real interest of a murder story lies in the motive. That's the thing."

"Nope. It's the cleverness of the detail work. The art of the criminal. Now, if I were going to commit a murder…."

"Heavens and earth, Val! What are you talking about? Drop it, any way, and listen to little Anna. I've thought up a name for this place."

"Number two thousand and six!" Loft groaned. "I pray Heaven may sometime send me a guest who does not requite my hospitality by offering me a 'name for my place'!"

The vivacious little blonde who had just come up on the terrace, accompanied by a big, good-natured looking man, sat on the arm of Loft's chair, as she insisted on her suggestion.

"You'll like this, Val, though. It's different from the Stonywolds and Ferndales that the herd invents. It's Valhalla! There, how's that?"

"Rotten!"

"Not a bit of it,—is it, Ned?" and Anna Knox appealed to her husband, whose talk with Loft she had interrupted.

"Pretty good," he responded; "I believe Valhalla means the place of departed spirits,—so, in a way, it's appropriate!"

"If you people stay much longer, mine will be entirely departed. But while I've a dram left,—I can take a hint." Loft leaned over to touch a bell button.

"Oh, Val, listen!" Anna went on. "It's the name,—don't you see? Valentine,—Val,—Hall,—Valhalla!"

"I heard you the first time," and Loft looked at her smilingly; "but, though I recognized the Val connection,—I didn't get the Hall part till you explained it. Almost like a charade."

"You are the most aggravating thing!" and Mrs. Knox favored him with her best pout.

Little Anna was one of the few perfect blondes Nature ever turned out. She needed no vanity-case, her face was like a Greuze pastel. Her shining hair, carelessly tucked up, nestled over her ears in loose, involuntary rings, not at all a rolled-up mass.

Dainty of flesh and blood, she was always perfectly togged, and today, in her white knitted silk sport suit, she seemed a morsel that any man might greedily devour.

Ned Knox looked at her adoringly, yet a trifle uneasily as she lounged nearer to Valentine Loft.

"Come here, Anna," he said, authoritatively, "come here and sit by me."

"Yes, dear, as soon as I make Val consent to my suggestion."

She lightly ran her fingers through the thick dark hair of Loft's restless head.

"Get out, Anna!" he growled; "get out! I'll murder you!"

"Come over here, Anna," said Angel Bob Baldwin, the man who had arrived with her.

Baldwin was a giant person of the Viking type, and by reason of his calm serenity and frequently upturned blue eyes was called Angel.

"But I've had you all the afternoon," Anna smiled; "I can have Ned all my life,—and I can only catch Val in an unoccupied moment, now and then, when Pauline doesn't see me."

"Just for that, you've got to go," and with a calm push, Loft gently dislodged her from her perch, whereupon, nothing dismayed, she went round and sat on the other arm of his chair.

But Anna's caprices were always smiled upon, and Loft offered her a cigarette.

The veranda gave West, and the disappearing sun touched the flowers, the trees and Anna's golden hair with a final blaze of glory. None of the three men could keep his eyes off her exquisite face, and though seemingly unconscious of this, she saw it, exultantly, and her vain little soul fairly lapped it up.

The "place" of Valentine Loft was a small estate in Westchester County, more noticeable for its quiet taste and comfortable appointments than for grandeur. He had guests much of the time, and always a group of people over the weekends.

Yet, though up to now, a bachelor's domain, Petticoat Rule was imminent, for in a few months Loft would marry Pauline Fuller, and into her capable hands would pass the household reins of government.

But no gracious chatelaine could improve on the kindly courtesy or thoughtful hospitality of Valentine Loft.

A good-looking chap of thirty-two, he was a man of varied interests and vocations. A lawyer first, but more or less of a dabbler in Real Estate, an architect of no small skill and a general financier. But his natural quickness of intellect and his achieved efficiency enabled him to have many irons in the fire, and keep them all hot. In his offices he was a General, commanding, inspiring, conquering. In his home, he was a delightful, debonair host, a man of the world, the flesh and the devil.

One of his most endearing traits was a broad, sweet tolerance that forgave idiosyncrasies and even defects in others, making allowance for their unfortunate lack of mental or psychical equipment. Yet there were a few things he could not condone or forgive. On these points he was so positive as to seem stubborn.

One of these was his attitude toward divorce. With the assuredness of the inexperienced, he held that once married was always married. So far did he carry this notion of his, that he rarely made friends of divorced people, and preferred not to meet them.

Some had jestingly told him that after his own marriage he might change his mind, but his cold reception of these pleasantries forbade their repetition.

His love for Pauline Fuller was the love of his life,—in it he had already put his whole soul, and Loft's was not a fickle nature.

Another fad of his was the value of inaction. He deplored waste motion, and held that far more was lost by effort than by restraint. A favorite maxim was: "Do nothing and all things will be done." This he had picked up in a book somewhere, and frequently quoted it. Though such a code might be dangerous to a less executive brain, to Loft it was wise counsel.

And seemingly, his plan worked. He seemed, indeed, to do nothing and yet, in his domain all things were done. His household mechanism was of the most smooth-running variety, and no incoming bride could hope to improve on it,—the most she might hope would be to keep it up to its present standards.

With his calm foresight, Loft felt sure that Pauline would do this, or if she didn't, she could be taught to.

And now Pauline was under his roof, spending a blissful fortnight, made possible by the chaperonage of little Anna Knox.

Though a few months younger than Pauline, Anna was a matron of three years' standing, and so, thoroughly equipped for the office of chaperon. To be sure, Mrs. Ned Knox had her own notions of these duties, but her presence gave the conventional sanction to Pauline's visit.

Pauline, tall, dark, beautiful, came out from the house, pausing a moment in the doorway to lift her straight, heavy black eyebrows at Anna's position.

"You!" she exclaimed, "you grasping cormorant! You have all the men in the world, and yet you must needs reach out after my one little ewe lamb! You go and read your prayer-book where it says, 'Keep my hands from picking and stealing'!"

"I wasn't hurting your lammie," and Anna rose slowly from Loft's chair arm, and went over to sit beside her husband. "Was I, Val?"

"I didn't know you were there," Loft returned, looking surprisedly at her, as he rose to arrange a seat for Pauline, and Anna made a face at him.

Tea was brought then, with other cups even more cheering, and as the shadows lengthened across the lawn and dusk began to fall, conversation lagged and there were frequent silences.

"I'm asked down to Wyngate for the weekend," Baldwin said.

"You can't go, Angel," Loft told him quickly. "I've more guests coming, and you must help bore them to death."

"But they asked me, and they said they were going to have a lot of interesting people there."

"Contradiction of terms. Interesting people don't come in lots. The other sort do."

"Why, Val, how you do make on!" cried Anna. "Haven't we a group of interesting people right here now?"

"No; Pauline is the only interesting one, and I wouldn't except her only she's my fiancée, and it seems as if I ought to."

"What a bear you are," and Pauline glanced at him amusedly. She was taller and more slender than most girls, and possessed of a lithe grace that made one want to watch her every motion. Her coloring was very black and very white, save where a slight touch of rouge showed on either cheek. Her dark eyes were almost sad in repose, but brightened to shining light when she became animated. Her smile was fleeting and adorable, and the look she gave Loft was enough to turn any man's head.

"I'm awfully alone," complained Angel Bob. "Here's Pauline making eyes at Val, while he wriggles with delight. Here's my little flirt Anna, gone back to her husband, and I've nobody to play with."

"Well you can't run off for the weekend," Val repeated. "I'll import one or two pretty girls for you to flirt with, and I'll allow Pauline and Anna to give you a daily dozen of their witching smiles and glances."

"Oh, Lord, don't overdo it!" and Baldwin flung up his hands.

"Pauline," Anna said, "what do you think these men were talking about when Bob and I came suddenly upon them a few moments ago? Just as we reached them, Val was saying, 'Now, when I commit my murder—'"

"Hold hard, there, Anna," Loft said; "I didn't put it quite like that. You see I've not yet fully decided to do one. As a matter of fact, I was saying, if I were going to commit a murder—"

"Well, what's the difference? They're both in the future tense."

"Finish your sentence, Val," observed Pauline. "It sounds interesting."

"You see, Ned and I were discussing Detective Stories. We're both fond of them."

"I thought nobody read them," interrupted Bob, "except English Premiers and American Presidents. I assumed they were rather highbrow stuff."

"Anything Bob says is funny," said Anna, and as he smirked complacently, she went on, "because he's so funny looking."

Whereupon Baldwin really did look funny.

"Go on, Val," commanded Pauline.

"Well, I'm always interested in the plans of the murderer. If I were one, I'd lay my plans and go about my work in such a careful and clever way, that the crime could never be brought home to me. It could never be discovered who did it."

"Then there wouldn't be any Detective Story," declared Mrs. Knox. "Moreover, Val, you couldn't do that,—it would be impossible."

"On the contrary it would be dead easy," contended Baldwin. "Why, I couldn't kill anybody because I'm too soft-hearted, but if I did, I'd easily arrange it so it would be an insoluble mystery."

"It isn't as easy as all that," Loft said, slowly; "it's possible, but difficult. You see, you have to guard against so many contingencies. And detectives are sharp chaps."

"In fiction," said Bob.

"In real life, too. Even if they don't do the Sherlock act, they very often bring home the bacon. Anyway, that would have to be reckoned with."

"What method is most approved this year?" Pauline asked, composedly.

"Strangling," said Bob, promptly. "Strangling is neat, clean and cool. Needs no weapon, leaves no mark. Try our strangulation method, you will never use any other!"

"That's all very well for you, with muscles like pile-drivers and hands like clam-rakes!" Knox looked at his own small and neatly cared-for hands.

He was a trifle undersized, but agile and athletic. In inverse proportion to his size his egotism was supreme, and he was opinionated and a bit cocky. His imagination was unlimited, and to its fullest scope he invented short stories which sold to the best magazines at the best prices.

"And yet, Bob," he went on, "I'd think your poetic soul would balk at strangling. It's not really artistic, you know."

"What is?" asked Anna.

"Shooting. That's a gentleman's method. Shoot your man,—quick,—ping!—all over."

"But the weapon?" said Loft, "how to conceal it?"

"There's where your cleverness gets in its fine work. I could do it. I could either cause the weapon to disappear,—or, with it, fasten the crime on another—oh, no, that way wouldn't do,—they'd see through that,—well, then suppose—"

Knox's voice drifted to incoherent mutterings. He was thinking up and rejecting one plan after another so rapidly that language could not keep pace with his inventive mind.

"He's off," said Loft, smiling. "He's in the throes of composition. But he's wrong, and so are you, Bob. Stabbing is the only thing. Then, you see,—"

"Oh, yes, I know," Bob growled. "Pick up the paper-cutter from the library table,—Florentine dagger sort of thing,—jab it in and leave it in the wound. Handkerchief wrapped round hand,—no fingerprints on aforesaid dagger. Butler down at seven A.M. Gives alarm—I always said, Val, you had no imagination. That's the most hackneyed plot of all."

"Needn't use paper cutter if you don't want to," said Loft, imperturbably. "Take dagger along, if you like. Or use jack-knife,—or carver,—or long clipping-shears."

"That's new," conceded Bob. "Clipping-shears are not hackneyed. Would you use 'em open or shut?"

"An open and shut case," said Knox, coming out of his reverie, but no one noticed him.

"You've omitted the best way of all," said Pauline, her slow smile and whimsical glance robbing her speech of horror. "That's poison."

"Too hard to procure," Knox said, thoughtfully. "Dramatic, in a way,—but not facile of achievement."

"Oh, stop this talk," and Anna shuddered. "You give me the willies!"

"Now, Anna, be reasonable," Bob admonished her. "To our class of mentality,—and you said, yourself we were all interesting people,—no subject is taboo. Beside, you must be interested in these themes. It's being done. Detective Fiction is no longer read solely by statesmen and College Professors. The movement has invaded the stage. Only sleuth plays are bought nowadays by our best managers."

"Don't talk more than you want to, Angel," Pauline said, kindly. "I'll relieve you for a while. Why, yes, Ned, one can get poison easily enough."

"But how? Its sale is prohibited—"

"But no prohibition ever really prohibited anything. It only makes it more difficult to come by—"

"And therefore, more attractive," suggested Loft. "I'm not surprised, though, Pauline, at your choice of method, for poison is preeminently a woman's way. You girls couldn't manage a shooting or a stabbing, nor, unless you've gone in strong for athletics, could you pull off a successful strangle,—but poison, now, ah, there you have it."

"There you don't have it," cut in Bob. "Notwithstanding Pauline's jaunty assurance, I'll bet no one of us interesting people here would know how to go about getting enough poison to kill a baby!"

"Oh, you have to know the chemist, I suppose, or have a club chum who knows him," Loft said; "of course, if I wanted poison I'd get it,—beyond all manner of doubt. But it implies premeditation and preparation and a certain intimacy with one's victim, and then there's always the vial to be disposed of."

"It might be a powder," said Pauline.

"You could eat the paper, if necessary," added Bob. "The vial of course you couldn't."

"More and better authors than ever are writing detective stories, aren't they?" Knox said. "I believe I'll try one."

"Short or long?"

"Have to be short,—Never write books. I say, that Curran chap is doing some corkers."

"Hugh Curran? Indeed he is! I've just read his 'Brick Walls' and 'Mystery of the Monastery,' and they're all a first rate Detective story ought to be." Bob spoke enthusiastically. "By Jove, I'd like to know that fellow."

"If you'll be a good boy and stay here this weekend, I'll invite him over," said Loft, smiling.

"Do you know him?" cried Anna. "Oh, do ask him! I never met a real author! Husbands don't count," and she flung a merry smile at Ned. "What's he like, Valentine?"

"I've only met him once,—at the Sports Club. But he seemed all there, and he's a friend of the Gedneys and the Bowles' so he must be righto. By the way, Angel, he's a book collector of great wealth, so you can put a few over on him. Rich book collectors never know anything."

"Don't they?" and Baldwin smiled.

Though not a regular book dealer, Angel Bob was a connoisseur, and negotiated personal orders for exceedingly rare and very expensive works. He had bought and sold more than one Folio Shakespeare and Gutenberg Fragment to his own advantage as well as that of his satisfied clients.

Imaginative, visionary, vague in many ways, Baldwin was of accurate and sure knowledge where Rares and Antiques were concerned. He loved the old books; the print, the paper, the bindings, all were of intense interest to him. He had bought several choice specimens for Loft, at attractive prices, and he had even sold a few things to Hugh Curran himself.

Not under his own name. As a matter of business policy, Angel Bob thought it no harm to use the fictitious firm name of Baldwin and Co.

But this was an open secret, and his friends often chaffed the Angel on his Trade. At which he good-naturedly smiled and continued his still hunt for special finds which he could buy for a song and sell for a chorus.

"Tell us about him,—what's he like?" begged Anna.

"I didn't notice him much,—it was a fortnight ago, before I'd read any of his books. It was at luncheon, and all I remember is that he salted every dish before he even tasted it."

"Poor compliment to the cook," said Pauline; "he might at least taste first, and give her the benefit of the doubt."

"No," Knox objected, "you don't see it right, Pauly. I'm sure he requires more salt than the average man, so he puts it in first. That, to my mind, is more polite than to taste, and then add salt. That seems a reproof. The first is merely a precaution, knowing his own idiosyncrasy."

"Oh, Ned! You and your psycho-analysis!"

"That isn't psych anything. It's imagination. Well, when we get Curran here we can ask him all about the best and cheapest modes of murder. By the way, I've heard that Curran isn't his real name. What is, Valentine?"

"I don't know. I think I was told, too, but I've forgotten. Everybody calls him Curran or Hugh."

"He hasn't been writing but a few years,—strange his pseudonym sticks to him so."

"He was a movie actor for a couple of years previous, I believe. He used the name of Hugh Curran there, too."

"I suppose few movie actors use their real names. What does he look like?"

"Oh, tall, dark, holler-eyed, cadaverous, lantern-jawed,—"

"I know what Val means!" giggled Anna, "he means he's tired of the subject!"

"Not quite that," Loft denied, "but I don't remember how he looked,—so I made him up. You'll see him in a few days,—can't you wait?"

"I can," Pauline said, quietly, "but I don't see, dear, why you want a moving picture actor here."

"Oh, he isn't that any more. He's now a prominent novelist and a popular author. Quite different, I assure you!"

"I'll ask him to teach Neddie to write stories," Anna declared, and returned her husband's scowl by a friendly kiss.

CHAPTER 2

A CELEBRATED GUEST

VALENTINE LOFT was of most courteous even genial demeanor, but he also had an air of dictatorship about him that somehow made any request of his seem a command. And this with no loss of courtesy or geniality, but rather with a potency that made his hearer eager to accede to his wishes.

The charm of Loft's personality was a variable factor. When he chose to exercise it, few could withstand its lure, but when he elected to be aloof or indifferent, he was so unresponsive as to be almost repellent.

It was with his most cordial smile that he said, "If you'll come for the weekend, Mr. Curran, we'll do all we can to entertain you, and I know you'll entertain us."

"That's fair enough," and Hugh Curran smiled back at him. "But how do you know what will entertain me?"

"Don't. But we've all sorts and conditions of amusements over home, and I'm guessing you'll be able to pick something to fit. Come, anyway."

Curran was not much given to accepting invitations to strange houses, for his ventures had not always proved satisfactory, but impelled by Valentine's insistence he considered the question, gazing meanwhile at his would-be host.

Hugh Curran was not at all the lean and lanky individual that Loft had jestingly pictured him. On the contrary, he was a bit thickset, though active and even athletic. His face was round and rosy, somewhat of the type of an English country squire, and his gray eyes had a humorous twinkle, though they were roving rather than straightforward.

His hair was sandy and not very abundant. If he had been a movie actor he was certainly no film hero; his was probably a character part.

"Many people there?" he asked, casually.

"Ten or a dozen. One's a Countess,—Russian."

"That doesn't intrigue me. Go on. Anyone I know?"

"Stella Lawrence? Psychic, ash-blonde—"

"Pah! Go on."

"Mr. and Mrs. Jack Meredith—"

"Don't know 'em."

"Mrs. Ned Knox,—gay little married flirt, pretty as a poet's dream,— Miss Pauline Fuller, my fiancée,—and that's all the women."

"Men?"

"Oh, come now,—aren't you a bit of a fuss?"

"No. Men?"

"Well, Ned Knox,—chum of mine; Bob Baldwin, ditto."

"Baldwin, the book dealer?"

"Yes."

"I'll come. I'm a collector, and he knows more about old books than any one I ever met."

"You know him, then?"

"In a booky way. I'd like to talk books with him. I'll come."

For once, Valentine Loft had a strange feeling of being favored by the visit of a guest. Usually it was the other way; but though the experience was novel it was not unpleasant. Indeed, he went so far as to say, "Thank you, I'm glad to have you. Come over in time for tea,—I'll send for your duffle."

The interview had taken place at the Club house, and as the two men separated, a man sitting nearby turned to Loft with a quizzical look.

"Surprised at you, old top!" he said, smiling. "Didn't know tuft-hunting was among your sports."

"If I choose," and Loft nodded indifferently. "But I asked him because the girls over at the house are crazy to meet him. And, too, he seems an interesting chap."

"Not that; but I know your whims, and Hugh Curran is a divorced man."

"He is! I didn't know that! What's his real name, by the way?"

"Don't remember,—Dyer or Dwyer, or something like that. He's always called Hugh Curran. Like O. Henry, you know. Few know *his* real name."

"I don't care anything about his name, but I wish I'd known he was a divorced man. I've a prejudice—"

"I know you have, but it's a silly one. In this day and generation you have to accept divorce as you do the universe. You needn't go in for it yourself, but you ought to respect the rights of those who do."

Jim Martin looked at Loft seriously. The men were good friends, and Martin was one of the few who ever presumed to reprove the autocrat.

"Perhaps I'm morbid on the subject, but I can't bring myself to treat it lightly."

"Don't treat it at all. Leave it lay. And especially in Curran's case. Why worry? He's an author and a celebrity—"

"Hardly that."

"Well, his detective stories are mighty popular, and that means celebrity nowadays. Anyway, he's important enough to have his personal affairs let alone."

"All right, I don't propose to discuss the thing with him. I'm sorry I asked him to my house, but it's done now, and can't be helped. At any rate he's presentable."

Loft went home, rather disgusted with himself for not having further investigated Curran's affairs before giving him an invitation. But since it couldn't be helped, he dismissed it from his mind.

"Is he coming?" cried Anna from the veranda, as Loft appeared.

"Yes, tonight,—he'll stay till Monday. Don't bowl him over completely, Anna."

"Why not?" and the seraph face looked innocently inquiring. "What's he look like, Val?"

"Elderly, stooping, rather rheumatic and with long white whiskers."

"Nonsense! You told a different story yesterday."

"And neither is true," Ned Knox said. "Wait till you see him, Anna. He's not nearly so good-looking as your own legitimate husband."

"Nobody is," and Little Anna beamed on the man who adored her so. "But I suppose he's a man of genius."

"They're terrors," observed Angel, from a swing in the corner of the porch, where he sat idly looking over one of Curran's books. "I've read Lombroso, and a man of genius is the most awful brute on the face of the earth."

"Heavenly!" cried Anna, "I love brutes! But why are men of genius 'em?"

"Because their brains hover between achievement and insanity. Don't you know, 'Great wits are sure to madness near allied, and thin partitions thought from sense divide.' Pope."

"You're in no danger of dementia, then," and Anna smiled kindly on him. "But all insane people aren't brutes. Some are quite gentle."

"What delightful subjects you choose for discussion," and Pauline came toward them. She usually was the last one to arrive as the group gathered for tea. Anna spitefully said it was to create a sensation by her appearance, but Pauline had replied that she always did that anyway. Whereupon Anna had sulked.

Pauline did, however, always command attention. Without effort, she seemed to dominate the rest, and though Anna was more beautiful from an artist's standpoint, yet a poet would find greater inspiration in Pauline's dark eyes and sensitive face than in Anna's pink and white Bisque beauty.

The two girls were not friends, although convention kept them kindly courteous. They had little in common, and were rarely alone together.

Yet both looked forward to the coming of the stranger. Anna, because he would be a new man to flirt with and an important one, Pauline because of a curiosity to see what he was like.

The house guests already arrived, flocked to the terrace where tea would be served.

A notable arrival was the Countess Galaski.

Unpretentious of appearance, the titled Russian was a general favorite. Sharp-tongued and sharp-witted, she yet had a superabundant sense of humor, and beneath all a kind heart. She jollied the men, admonished the women, took always the best of everything for herself, and was always happy.

"How are you?" she cried, looking about inclusively, as she stepped through the doorway. "I am here! Angel, the best chair! Valentine, a foot cushion! Pauline, you have gone off in your looks! Fie, fie! Anna, I will not speak to you,—you are too beautiful. Come here, and kiss me."

"Who, me?" inquired Knox, rushing to her.

"Yes, bad man, you!" she held up her rouged cheek for a somewhat crestfallen caress from Knox, who had expected rebuff. But the Countess never did the expected.

Then Stella Lawrence trailed in. Stella was the sort who always trails in preference to any other means of locomotion. Though her skirts did not quite touch the ground, there were ends of chiffon, floating draperies and a long filmy scarf that trailed along the floor behind her.

Green-eyed, ash-blonde, pale, thin, willowy, she paused back of the chair of the rather robust and florid countess, well knowing the value of the contrast.

"Get away!" Countess Galaski screamed. "Get away, you and your Burne-Jonesiness! I can't stand the comparison!"

"Indeed you can, Countess," Anna declared, cattily. "It makes you look awful wholesome and real."

"In for a high old time, ain't we?" whispered Roly Mears to Pauline.

This delightful young man was very young and very incorrigible.

He said what he chose, and though, having never met a countess before, he was not a bit scared of her, it was dawning on him that they might yet become cronies.

"You behave yourself, Roly," Pauline returned. "There's mischief in the air. Anna's on her high horse—"

"And Stella's full of the devil, and if Friend Countess puts up a chattering, there'll be fireworks."

"Hush, here are the Merediths."

The Merediths were scarcely worth hushing for, being the colorless pair that seem to infest house-parties unavoidably.

Comfortably middle-aged, inconspicuous of dress, pleasantly chatty of manner, the two melted into the group and were lost to notice.

And then Hugh Curran came.

Though nearly everyone present would have scorned to admit any awe of the celebrity, yet a slight hush fell as the author greeted his host.

The Countess stared openly. Anna donned her coyest smile, and Stella Lawrence fell quickly into what she deemed her most fetching pose.

Roly Mears stopped short in the middle of a funny story and even Pauline, who was presiding at the table, allowed the cup she was filling to run over.

Graceful and at ease, Hugh Curran moved about until he was made acquainted with all, and then looking around a bit deliberately, chose a seat by the Countess.

Roly Mears, cup in hand, joined them.

"I say, Mr. Curran," he began, "I've read your books,—I think they are fine—"

"Roly, you baby," the Countess cried; "that isn't the way to talk to a real author. That's only for the little upstarts who like to hear about their 'published works.' Mr. Curran is above and beyond that sort of thing."

"Thank you, Countess," said the author, gratefully; "if you can manage it, I'd like you to travel round with me and make that speech everywhere, just before I arrive."

"I ought to be chagrined," Roly admitted, "but I'm not. I'm fascinated,—with both of you. What are you going to talk about, Mr. Curran? Politics?"

"No, indeed," and Hugh Curran smiled. "I'm not going to talk at all. I'm going to listen."

"To me," said Ned Knox, joining them. "You needn't talk about your own books, Mr. Curran, but do settle a vexed question we were discussing the other day. Is motive or method a more important factor in a detective story?"

Curran looked a bit bored, but answered with evident patience.

"I think that is entirely a matter of opinion with both author and reader. Some are more interested in one, some in the other."

"After all there are only three motives," Meredith said, sententiously, "greed, revenge and love."

He had quite evidently heard or read this statement, and pronounced it as a great truth.

"Haven't you omitted an important one?" asked Curran, quietly. "Isn't fear sometimes an impelling motive?"

"Fear? Of what?"

"Fear of harm from the victim, fear of revelation of a secret,—" Curran let his gaze wander round the room. Clearly, he was not interested in this talk.

He looked at his beautiful hostess. Pauline sat still at the tea table, her hands clasped in her lap, her eyes, with a far away look gazing out of the window, across the lawn. She, too, was uninterested.

Angel Bob, pacing up and down the terrace, was listening.

"I've no use for detective stories," the Countess said, bluntly; "I detest them. A good old fashioned love story for me. But, if I do read a murder yarn, what I like best is the finding of those funny little clues. Cigarette stubs, with the criminal's monogram; a broken cuff-link, an initialled handkerchief,—ah, those are the things that you can't get along without,—eh, Mr. Curran?"

"They are certainly useful," he smiled. "But of late years we try to do without the broken cuff-link or the dropped handkerchief."

"Is that what you call circumstantial evidence?" Stella Lawrence trailed over to the novelist. "Just what is circumstantial evidence, Mr. Curran?"

She put the question as one of magnificent import. Stella was like that. She cared nothing at all for detective fiction, but if she asked a question concerning it, she fully expected detailed information.

She got it.

"It's this way, Miss Lawrence," Curran said, his tone a bit patronizing. "I'll illustrate it by an anecdote. An old darkey was arrested for stealing chickens, and he was convicted on circumstantial evidence. 'What's circumstantial evidence?' a neighbor asked him. 'Well,' he said, 'ez near ez I kin splain it f'um de way it's been splained to me, circumstantial evidence is de feathers dat you leaves lyin' roun' after you has done wid de chicken.' That, Miss Lawrence, is practically what circumstantial evidence is. Or, rather, the clues that detectives set so much by, are merely feathers left around."

"Oh, how graphic!" and Stella clasped her hands delightedly; "and how wonderfully well you do dialect. Are you a Southerner, Mr. Curran?"

"No," he returned, "I'm from Indiana."

"Of course," exclaimed Roly Mears, "where else could a real author come from?"

But Curran made no reply. Again his glance roved toward Pauline, who, though not yet chatelaine in name, assumed the position of hostess.

She raised her eyes and met his and quickly looked down again. Pauline had not the heedless effrontery of Anna, nor yet the calm poise of Countess Galaski.

Mrs. Meredith, the busybody! sitting next to Pauline, whispered, roguishly. "Don't be so embarrassed, my dear, because a stranger shows his admiration. You are looking unusually lovely today."

Whereupon Pauline blushed almost vividly, and the perspicacious Hugh Curran smiled.

"Will you take me on at croquet, Stella?" asked Mears, "you can trail round at that in those swishy draperies very effectively. And you couldn't golf or bowl or tennis in them."

"Yes, Roly,—get two more—"

"No; I want you all to myself."

"Is that the way one does here?" asked Curran, quickly. "Then, Miss Fuller, will you walk with me,—and may I have you all to myself?"

"You may not!" and Valentine Loft spoke decidedly. "But, perhaps Mr. Curran, you do not know that Miss Fuller is my fiancée. I allow no man to have her 'all to himself.'"

"And quite right," Curran bowed. "Pardon me if I was indiscreet. Mrs. Knox, will you walk with me—round the gardens?"

"All to yourself?" and Anna tilted her head and smiled up from under her long lashes.

"Yes,—if your husband will allow—"

"He doesn't allow me anything,—except a quarterly. I'm a twentieth century wife, and I do my own sweet will. Come along, Mr. Curran. Good-by, Ned." She tossed her husband a kiss, and turned toward the steps.

Angel Bob Baldwin followed her.

"I'm with you two," he announced, cheerfully. "I'm the three that makes the crowd."

"Come on, Mr. Baldwin," said Curran, so heartily that Anna bit her lip in annoyance. Had she then, made no impression on the lion's heart?

Her annoyance increased as they proceeded along the garden paths, for save for an occasional and almost perfunctory speech to her, the two men talked continuously of rare books and their authors.

"You're still collecting Incunabula?" Baldwin asked, and Curran replied in enthusiastic affirmative.

Then the talk touched upon Elzevirs and Bodinis, on Kelmscott Press and Doves Bindery, until Anna rebelled.

"You must either stop that Choctaw," she decreed, "or take me back to the house! I won't be brought out here in this rose-scented dusk by two good-looking men, and have the talk entirely over my head! You ought to be ashamed! It isn't done!"

There was a pathetic note in her voice, a hint of tears, and each man felt guilty. Immediately they dropped the subject of books; Curran forbore to mention the work that he was about to discuss, and Angel deferred the account of a rare bargain he had lately acquired, till some more convenient time.

"Tell us all about yourself, Mr. Curran," Anna said, by the way of a starter. "Are you engaged to be married?"

"No, indeed, why should I be?"

"Foolish question, Number 1008! Why should you not be? You are depriving some nice girl of a perfectly good husband."

"Oh, I'm not perfectly good,—I'm indifferent bad. And, too, I've been married once."

"You have! Oh," Anna's voice became very tender, "forgive me. Has she been dead long?"

"She isn't dead at all. Did you never hear of Reno?"

"I have—indirectly. So that's the way it is."

"I say, Curran," and Angel Bob looked at him earnestly, "does Loft know this?"

"I don't know, I'm sure. Probably he does,—it's no secret. Why?"

"Only that he has had a special, almost an abnormal hatred of divorce and of divorced people. As a friend, let me ask of you not to say anything on the subject to him."

"I shan't purposely,—certainly. But what a queer notion. One might as well have a prejudice against blue-eyed men,—or against maple trees. Statistics prove—"

"Oh, we know all that," said Anna, impatiently, "and it isn't a question of divorce at all. It's a question of humoring Val's whims. And I don't mind telling you that your stay here will be a whole lot pleasanter if you don't touch on that subject."

"I surely agree. Any other subject taboo?"

"Not by him," Anna assured him. "But if you care to consider poor little me, I'll beg of you not to talk collecting *all* the time. Something tells me that when you all get started, say after dinner, tonight, you'll begin by looking over Val's collections,—he hoards lots of things beside books and you'll talk antiques and curios and bindings and such things—and I do hate 'em so!"

"Never mind, Little Anna, if they begin on that, I'll take you off somewhere in the moonlight and flirt with you."

Angel looked into her eyes with a glance that was not all make-believe.

"I appreciate that, Bob, for I know the old things interest you, too."

"Only the books, Anna. I don't care a rap for Val's Egyptian stuff—or Mexican. I do care for books though."

"And you hate to see them maltreated, eh, Mr. Baldwin?" Curran looked at him quizzically. "You'd hate to see a rare old volume torn or injured, wouldn't you?"

"It would be sacrilege," Angel said, emphatically.

"Imagine tearing out a leaf!" and Curran almost shuddered.

"Why, who would do such a thing as that?" cried Baldwin.

"The subject is taboo, remember," and then Curran addressed himself to Anna.

CHAPTER 3

THE TRAGEDY

DINNER at Valhalla that night was a brilliant affair.

Anna's name for the place had caught on, and Loft began to like it as he heard it used by his guests.

Anna, as chaperon, graced the head of the table, and Curran sat at her right hand. This left Pauline for Loft's guest of honor, and as she took her place beside him, he thought she had never looked more beautiful. Her great dark eyes seemed brighter than usual and her cheeks showed a flush that was quite obviously not rouge. She wore black, her only ornament a long slender neck-chain of small bright diamonds. She was in vivacious, almost perverse mood, quite unusual for the calm, gracious Pauline.

Anna, tonight, was demure and coy. She set herself the task of subjugating Hugh Curran, and so far as she could see she was putting it over.

Yet the man was tricky, she could see that, and more than likely, she thought, his devotion was insincere.

Though commonplace looking, Curran had an air of easy superiority that made him almost distinguished. But his round red face and sparse sandy hair precluded all pretension to good looks.

Countess Galaski was gorgeous. Robed in white satin, glittering with jewels and autocratic of manner, she appropriated the best of everything, was rude to everybody, and yet somehow charmed all by her gay naïveté.

Stella wore especially long and diaphanous draperies, of pale green and silver, and looked more than ever like the Blessed Damosel.

On the whole Loft had a right to feel proud of his guests, for aside from their appearance they were a group of mentally alert and even original talkers.

But when the Countess began to expatiate on her marvelous collection of miniatures, Anna gayly called a halt.

"Countess, darling," she said, "we beg of you to don't. Mr. Curran is a book collector and he's crazy to talk Black Letters, or whatever they are, with Angel Bob, who is an Old Book Fiend too. Val, of course, collects everything, from books to old bandboxes, and I believe Mrs. Meredith collects postcards. But they've all promised not to talk Collect at the table. So, be goody-girl, Countess dear, and drop your miniatures."

"Oh, very well," and the Countess smiled at Little Anna, "the loss is yours not mine. But I have to talk. I'll tell you about—"

"Wait a minute," the incorrigible Roly dared to interrupt her, "since we have Mr. Curran here, and Lord knows when I'll ever get a chance at him again, let's talk Detective Stories. We all love 'em."

"Not all of us," Anna dissented; "but you may talk on that subject for fifteen minutes, Roly. After that, I shall choose the theme."

"To go back to a discussion we had the other day," Angel Bob began, "what do you think the best and finest method of murder, Mr. Curran?"

Mrs. Meredith gave a little gasp at this, and her husband looked shocked. But Curran took it as a matter of course.

"Each method has its advantages," he began. "And too, much depends on the criminal. If he has any surgical training, stabbing is indicated, if he has a good aim, shooting is better. An athlete would, of course, strangle."

"And a woman would give poison," said Pauline, slowly.

"Yes," and Hugh Curran looked at her, "yes, a woman probably would."

"If this conversation keeps up," Mrs. Meredith spoke hysterically, "I shall have to leave the table."

"Don't be a fool, Madame!" exclaimed the Countess. "If you would read De Quincey's essay on Murder As A Fine Art, you would learn that the greatest minds are willing to discuss such matters. One does not have to be a spook to discuss Spiritualism!"

"Spiritualism is a decent subject," Mr. Meredith said; "whereas, murder is, or should be, outside the pale of our thoughts."

"Well, you have to be dead before you can be a spirit," the Countess returned, "and if one is unfortunate enough to be murdered, there's no reason why those still alive shouldn't talk about it."

"I'm for strangling," Baldwin said; "then there's no weapon,—no 'feathers left around,' you see. Also, granting one *wants* to kill a man, what a pleasure it must be to feel one's fingers on his throat,—tightening, closing in—tighter,—a gasp—"

Angel Bob, in mischievous mood, portrayed his speech in dumb show, with such realism that Mrs. Meredith shrieked and rose from the table.

"Sit down" commanded the Countess, in ringing tones, and Mrs. Meredith sat down.

"I'd shoot," and Ned Knox, picking up the theme, acted the part of an intruder, taking aim at an unsuspicious victim. He chose Loft for his purpose, and aimed a fork carefully at his right temple.

"But I can see you," Loft objected.

"Turn your head away, then," Knox counselled.

"Shooting has disadvantages," Curran said, musingly. "There's the noise."

"Silencer," returned Knox.

"Not always practicable. Then, there's the weapon."

"Easy enough to dispose of," Knox laughed, "except in fiction, where it is needed as a clue,—if it has initials on it, or is one of a pair."

"Righto!" and Curran laughed appreciatively. "I'm glad to learn how you readers are on to our hackneyed tricks. Stabbing is a good way—"

"Yes," Loft agreed; "with the library paper-cutter. Used to be an old Italian dagger, and the victim many times said it ought not to be left around, as it was a suggestion and a temptation to any murderous-minded bystander."

"Oh, Lord, you know all the tricks of the trade!" Curran sighed in mock despair. "I confess it's hard to get a novelty for a story nowadays."

"But it's easy to murder," said Bob.

"It isn't," contended Loft; "it's possible, but it's a delicate and difficult affair to put over artistically. I'm not talking of yeggs and gunmen."

"Except for them, it's impossible." Ned Knox averred. "I don't propose to try it for that reason. I know I'd fail."

"Of course you would," and Anna giggled. "If you could put it over, you'd have tried it on me long ago. I've given you sufficient provocation, I know. Anyway, time's up,—No more murder talk. Now, we'll discuss Mr. Curran. How do you all like him?"

"Top hole!" cried Roly Mears. "But I want to know more about him. What does he eat for breakfast? What—"

"Wait till morning and you'll find that out," Loft interrupted. "I want to know his real name. No secret, is it, Mr. Curran?"

"Not a bit. I had another name, but I lost it, somehow. It's my besetting sin,—to lose things. I lost my wife, then I lost my ambition. I found that again, though. But mostly I lose material things. I can't keep a pencil or a rubber or a sheet of paper, no matter how many I buy. I'm just naturally untidy. My room always looks like Broadway the day after Election night. My brushes just won't stay on my dresser; my clothes crawl out of their wardrobes and drawers. I can't help it,—are you like that, Miss Fuller?"

Apparently he addressed Pauline because she was looking at him intently, seemingly interested in his tale of his personal derelictions.

"N—no," she replied, looking startled at being thus spoken to. "I don't think so,—I—I never thought about it."

"Goodness, Pauline," said Anna, staring at her, "don't take it so seriously. I can vouch for your tidiness. I never knew a girl who kept her top bureau drawer in order as well as you do."

"That is a sure test," declared the Countess. "I'll bet Miss Lawrence's is a kaleidoscope of laces and ribbons, gloves and handkerchiefs."

"It is!" said Stella, good-naturedly. "And I want it so—With my temperament, I couldn't be methodical or systematic or anything like that. Fate rules me—"

"And you leave it to Fate to clear up your bureau drawers," said Roly, laughing. "Good idea, so do I."

"I don't," said Mrs. Meredith primly, but no one seemed to care deeply.

The Merediths were out of place, but had been asked because of some social obligation of Loft's. They were shocked several times during dinner, but perhaps Mrs. Meredith's sensibilities were most greatly jarred, when, leaving the dining room, she chanced to overhear Hugh Curran ask the butler for a toothpick.

The capable Binns didn't allow himself to be jarred, but he was bothered, for the request caught him unprepared. However, he quickly bethought himself of the tiny Japanese wooden toothpicks that the cook used to pin rolled morsels and he soon supplied the distinguished guest.

Angel Bob noticed the incident and was more amused at Mrs. Meredith's disdain than at Curran's unconventionality.

The party broke up into smaller groups.

Anna seized upon Curran, who went, nothing loath, with her to see the moonlight from the upper terrace.

Loft and Pauline went for a stroll in the rose garden; Roly Mears set himself to tease Stella and to please the Countess, succeeding well with both.

As it neared bedtime, all gathered for good-nights in the library.

"Tomorrow," said Curran, as he looked at the filled shelves, "I want to spend the morning in here. You have wonderful treasures, Mr. Loft, and I anticipate joyous hours with them."

"I am clairvoyant, Mr. Curran," Stella said, looking at him dreamily, "and I can read your soul."

"Good Heavens, don't, Miss Lawrence! It's not fit reading for a young girl!"

"But I'm not like other girls," Stella was determined to have her innings, "I'm apart,—alone."

"Yes?" said Curran, not thinking of anything better to say.

"Yes. And in your soul I read a longing for all that is beautiful and good—"

"I like them beautiful,—I'm not so insistent on the good," and Curran smiled. This line of talk always bored him.

"Things, I mean, not people. Oh, I can read you, Mr. Curran."

"And I can read you, Miss Lawrence. I'm clairvoyant, myself."

"Oh, are you?" cried the Countess. "Read us all, won't you? I don't care for Stella's foolishness,—you shut up, Stella."

"Want a table?" asked Loft, "or any paraphernalia?"

"Oh, I'm not a parlor Magician," Curran protested. "I don't know anything about legerdemain or hocus-pocus. But I have a natural gift of reading minds."

"Don't do it!" exclaimed Roly Mears. "If these people know what I'm thinking they'd never speak to me again!"

"You're joking," said Curran, "but there are some really quaking in their shoes, lest I tell something they don't want told."

"I know!" said the Countess, "it's Mrs. Meredith! I always suspected she led a double life! Well, much as I want to know the truth about it, I beg of you, Mr. Curran, don't tell it all out in public."

Mrs. Meredith blushed angrily, but said nothing. She had learned it was better not to irritate Countess Galaski.

"Go on," urged Anna. "Tell us something to prove your powers. I hate people who say they can do things and then do nothing at all!"

"Yes," said the Countess, "go on! Tell anything you like about me."

"Very well," said Curran, "you're thinking that you wish you had worn your old slippers after all, for the new ones are a bit tight and they do pinch."

"You're perfectly right!" and the Countess joined in the general merriment. "But that isn't clairvoyance. I've had my face screwed up with pain all the evening!"

"Well, how's this, then? In the mind of one of you is a most disquieting thought, which I may suggest by *Black Pansy*."

"That's me!" said Ned Knox, as Curran waited for some response. "I've a lot of stock in that mine, and unless she picks up soon, I'll probably start 'Over the hills to the poorhouse!'"

"How did you know it, though?" and Anna looked at Curran, incredulously.

"Clairvoyance," replied Curran, not caring to say that he had seen a newspaper thrown down, with a marked notice about the mine.

"Also," he went on, "as I look around, I feel vibrations from others of you."

He glanced from one face to another, all breathlessly watching him.

"If I should say," he spoke very slowly, "if I should say *Rosalie*—would I reflect the word in anybody's mind?"

A dead silence followed.

Removing their regard from Curran, one looked at another, but no one spoke.

Nor did any one look especially self-conscious. Loft looked inquiring, Angel looked bewildered. The women looked merely interested, except Pauline, who seemed bored. She moved restlessly, and stared hard at Curran.

"Right," Curran said; "it's better not to recognize the reference." He nodded his head as in satisfaction.

"Suppose I say, '*Mr. S.*'" he went on. "Is he in any one's thoughts?"

Again the silence fell.

Anna, frankly curious, glanced quickly from one to another. From the faces, as she read them, the reference might mean something to Valentine Loft or to Bob Baldwin. On the other hand, they might look disturbed, as they both did, merely from interest in the proceedings.

"Oh, well," Curran resumed, "I see, the people who recognize my allusions prefer not to say so. I don't blame them. Now, Mrs. Knox, shall I tell what's in your mind? Shall I mention the name of—"

"No!" screamed Anna, "no! If you do, I'll kill you!"

But she told her husband afterward that she only said this to make a sensation.

"Then," said Curran, "I'll read Miss Lawrence's mind. Last night Miss Lawrence dreamed—"

"Stop!" Stella cried, her eyes staring; "if you dare divulge that dream—"

Curran smiled. He had made a stab in the dark, feeling sure that the psychic Stella, would always be dreaming and interpreting her dreams according to Freud.

"Guess we've had enough of this sort of thing," and Loft rose. "Don't trouble yourself, Mr. Curran, to read my mind, I can read it for myself."

"Nothing startling in it just now," Curran said; "but there will be soon. I'm slightly prophetic as well as clairvoyant, and I prognosticate a lot of surprising, even tragic thoughts for your mind soon."

"All right, I'll go to bed and sleep while the sleeping's good, then," and Loft inaugurated good-nights, and the party dispersed.

By next morning Loft had forgotten the irritation he felt at Curran's strange speech, and after his breakfast he went to the library to await the coming of his guest to talk books.

The women breakfasted in their rooms, the men dropping into the breakfast room whenever they pleased.

Loft was down first, but was soon joined by Angel and Ned Knox, both of whom wanted to hear Curran discourse on the subject of rare books.

"Keep your ears open, Bob, and find out what he wants," advised Loft. "You ought to be able to make a sale or two."

"Hope so," Bob assented. "He wants only Incunabula, though, and that's not so easy come by just now."

But the hours passed, and no sign of Hugh Curran.

At last, Loft, looking at the clock, said, "I'm annoyed. I have to go over to the Club before luncheon, and the time is growing short. I've a notion to send for Curran. I don't believe he's still asleep."

The butler was despatched to learn as to this, and was directed to be discreet.

Discretion itself, Binns returned to say that he could hear no sound from Mr. Curran's room and that though he had softly tried the door, it was locked.

They waited another half hour, and then Loft said, nervously, "You don't suppose anything has happened, do you? Maybe the man is ill."

"Nonsense," said Knox, "Men don't get ill overnight. He looked a healthy chap."

"All the same, I'm going up myself," and Loft went out to the hall.

He soon returned, saying, "There must be something the matter. I knocked and even pounded on his door, but got no response. I even listened at the keyhole, and I couldn't hear any breathing. Do you suppose he left in the night?"

"Through the window?" asked Angel.

"Well, it's queer. If we can't get anything from him, I'm going to break in."

"Oh, don't do that!" cried Knox. "Send Binns up outside—to the windows, you know."

"Can't,—it's so high."

"Ladder?"

"Yes,—but—oh, I suppose it's all right."

But after another hour, Loft declared he was going to get into that room.

"I'm responsible for him," he said; "he's my guest, and if he's merely sound asleep, he can't do more than curse me for my intrusion."

No response being made to continued knockings, and no sound heard by any of them listening, Loft ordered Binns to get a ladder and climb up to the window.

The butler did so, and returned to say that he could see Mr. Curran, fully dressed, sitting in an arm chair. The window was fastened. "Should he break in?"

"Yes, by the door," said Loft, suddenly determined. "That man must have had a stroke or something, if he's still dressed. In his evening togs, Binns?"

"Yes, sir."

"To work, then. You and I, together."

Loft and the butler put their shoulders to the bedroom door, and after one or two efforts burst through.

Hugh Curran sat in an arm chair, slightly relaxed in posture and as they immediately discovered, stone dead. The body was cold, proving he had died some hours previous.

The four men looked at him and at each other.

"Method?" asked Ned Knox, grimly.

Loft looked about him.

"I don't see any weapon," he said, shuddering, "but we can't think about that now. There's too much to do. Binns, call up Doctor Gilvray."

"What earthly good can a doctor do?" asked Angel, his blue eyes staring at the dead man.

"We have to have him," returned Loft, positively.

"Yes," agreed Knox, "he can tell whether it's natural death, accident, suicide or murder."

Angel looked at him curiously as he glibly rolled off these possibilities.

"Then," Loft went on, "we must call the police—"

"Not unless the doctor says so," put in Angel. "If he says it's a stroke—"

"That's so, we'll wait for his report. Now, the worst is, telling the women. Ned, you tell Anna and let her tell the others. No, she's too emotional. Here's a better plan. Angel, you ask the maids to get the Countess to give you an interview. Then you tell her about it, and let her tell Stella and the Merediths. I'll tell Pauline, myself."

"Are the girls up?"

"They'd better get up. The housekeeper can tell them to do so, but let them hear of the—this—from one of us."

"I suppose there'll be fainting and hysterics," said Bob, apprehensively, as he started on his unhappy errand.

"Maybe,—from Stella. Not the others," said Knox. "I won't let Anna make a scene,—not outside our rooms, anyway."

The two men went away, and Binns having gone to telephone, Valentine Loft was left alone with his dead guest.

He looked about the room. It was clear that Curran had not begun to get ready for bed. He had not even removed tie or collar.

Yet the room was in disorder. Near the dead man's chair were two books on the floor, several newspapers, a few scattered cigar ashes, some bits of torn paper, two lead pencils,—

Loft's mental cataloguing of these articles was interrupted by the arrival of the doctor.

CHAPTER 4

THE MEREDITH STORY

"WHO is this man?" asked Doctor Gilvray, sharply, as he strode across the room to look for himself on the dead man's features.

"Hugh Curran," Loft answered, briefly. "A fairly well-known author of fiction—"

"Yes, yes, I know Curran,—sleuth stories,—good ones, too. H'm,—been dead several hours,—six or eight, surely. Bad symptoms—"

"What do you mean by symptoms?" Loft showed an eager curiosity.

"Look at his face—cyanotic. Eyes wide open,—signs of bloody froth on his lips,—teeth tight clenched,—this man—" the doctor stopped to sniff at Curran's mouth,—"yes, this man died of poison,—Hydrocyanic acid. Suicide?"

"Good Lord, I don't know!" Valentine Loft stared. "I scarcely know him at all,—but, no,—I'm sure he wouldn't commit suicide,—he had all sorts of things to live for!"

"Well—well,—let's look further. Ah, yes, yes,—it's Prussic acid, for sure. There's a distinct odor of it on his lips. So, he either took the stuff voluntarily,—or, it was administered by someone else."

"But—" Loft looked puzzled. "But the room was locked."

"That would argue suicide,—but then, I see no container, do you? The poison must have acted instantaneously, and he would have had no more than time to fling away the paper or bottle,—scarcely that. He would more likely have dropped it where he sat. Has any one interfered with the room in any way?"

"No one. I've been here alone ever since we discovered this. And I've touched nothing,—nothing at all."

"There'll have to be an autopsy,—and, of course, you realize, Mr. Loft, it's a case for the police. I shall have to notify them at once."

"Oh, what a horrible situation. I've a house party here,—and, aside from that, I don't want my home invaded by a lot of snooping detectives—and all for a perfect stranger."

"How'd he happen to be here?"

"The people felt interested in him,—as a sort of celebrity,—and I asked him for a weekend visit. See here,—if anybody did for him, how did the intruder get in? We had to break in this morning."

"One of those seemingly insoluble mysteries of entrance, that always proves to be a simple matter after all. Any of the servants have a pass key?"

"No; and, anyway, the key was in the lock."

"Well, that's outside my jurisdiction. I'll have Detective Kinney put on this,—he's a sharp one. Now, get your household together,—say, in the library, and I'll have to question them pretty closely."

"Awful nuisance,—but I know it must be done. I wish I'd never seen Hugh Curran!"

"Where is his home? Where are his people?"

"I don't know. He hails from Indiana, but I think he lives in New York just now. The Club people will know all about him. Now, Doctor, Miss Fuller, my promised wife, is staying here. I want to tell her of this matter myself. And,—I wish you could excuse her from the general inquiry—"

"Can't be done. Must have everybody present, servants and all. I daresay some can be quickly dismissed, but I must get all the testimony possible. It's a strange case, I think,—though it may turn out a simple matter after all. Go ahead, Mr. Loft, and tell the lady about it, and I'll call Police Headquarters and get busy at once. Is there a telephone in the hall? Yes? Well, I'll lock this room door against my return. Oh, the lock is fairly burst off! Never mind,—I can keep my eye on it. I don't want anyone meddling in there."

"Here's Baldwin," Loft said, as they met Bob in the hall. "Mount guard in Curran's room, Angel, while the doctor is telephoning."

"Don't like the job, but I'll do it," Baldwin said, a rueful look on his usually smiling face. "Hurry up all you can, Doctor."

Loft went away to seek Pauline. He found her in the pretty sitting room that belonged to her suite, and though she had not yet been told of the tragedy, she knew from various unexplained stirrings about the house that something had happened.

"What is it, Val?" she asked, "what has happened?"

Gently he told her the bare facts as he knew them. He had feared she would be greatly shocked, possibly hysterical, but he was not prepared for the utter prostration that overtook her.

She gasped, choked for breath and almost fainted.

"No, don't call anybody," she asked, as he started for the door. "I'll be all right in a minute. Why—who—who did it?"

"Pauline, darling, we don't know that anybody did. It may be the man took his own life. Doctor Gilvray isn't certain. And maybe it's a stroke of some sort. Gilvray thought he detected the odor of bitter almonds, but I couldn't notice it. And the room was locked, and there's no bottle or paper to be found,—so I'm inclined to think it may have been a stroke."

"Do you?" Pauline gazed into his eyes. "Do you, really, Val?"

"Yes, dear, I do. But why are you so concerned? To be sure the occurrence itself is awful,—coming as it does during this visit of yours, that was to be such a gay, happy party. But aside from that, you've no personal interest in Curran, have you?"

"Oh, no, no. Of course not. How could I have? I saw him for the first time yesterday,—*yesterday*."

"That is so, dear, isn't it? You never saw Hugh Curran before?"

"I never laid eyes on Hugh Curran until yesterday," she averred, almost solemnly, and with a straightforward gaze at Loft. "And I hope I need never lay eyes on him again."

"No, sweetheart, no, of course not. We will have—him taken away just as soon as possible. But,—I'm sorry,—you'll have to come downstairs now, and answer a few questions the Examiner will ask you."

"Oh, no, Valentine! I can't,—I *can't*! Don't make me do that! Please, please, dear, if you love me,—don't make me do that!"

"I'm not making you, Pauline,—I tried to get you off. But it is imperative,—it is the law—"

"I don't care if it is the law,—I can't I—can't—" she broke into deep, silent sobbing.

"My precious girl, I'd save you this ordeal if it were in any way possible to do so. But it isn't. The detective will come up here if you don't go down. And think, Pauline, it isn't any more than the rest will do. Anna, Stella, the Countess, the Merediths,—all of us have to do the same. You will be asked only a few perfunctory questions,—it will be over in a few minutes. Whereas," he looked stern, "whereas dear, if you refuse, it will look strange,—even—suspicious—"

"Oh, of course I'll go, Val. I'll do whatever you tell me to. I only felt scared and horrified at first. Shall we go now?"

Suddenly Pauline had regained her poise, and was her own calm self again. She turned to Loft, her sweet face submissive, even willing to obey his request.

"Yes, come now. The others are gathered, I daresay. Don't talk much, Pauline. Just answer what they ask, carefully and concisely."

"Why, Val, what do you mean? Is there any—any danger—"

"No, of course not. But it's never wise to dilate on the subject you're asked about. However, tell all you know, of course."

"I'll glance at you, and if I'm doing all right you nod. If not shake your head."

"Very well. Oh, I'm so sorry, Pauline, that you must do this."

"Never mind, it's all right. Come along."

Together they went downstairs.

Their interview had been longer than Loft realized, and the household had assembled in the library.

The whole atmosphere of the house seemed changed.

Pauline had shuddered as they passed an officer in the hall, and another was to be seen patrolling the front terrace.

In the library Doctor Gilvray and Detective Kinney were ready to begin their inquiries.

"We needn't be over formal," the Doctor said. "First, Mr. Loft, you will tell all you know of Hugh Curran and how he came to be your guest."

Valentine Loft stated clearly and concisely the little he knew of the author, and explained that he had invited him merely because his guests were interested and also because Mr. Curran had expressed a desire to talk with Mr. Baldwin on the subject of old and rare books.

"He wanted to see your collection too, Val," Angel put in, as if disclaiming the entire responsibility.

"Yes,—he said he meant to spend this morning in the library," Loft returned, looking about him in rather an awed way.

"Then that doesn't point to a suicide," said the Detective, quickly.

"No, and it wasn't a suicide," Doctor Gilvray declared. "The man was murdered."

At this Anna gave a gasp of horror, and clutched at her husband's arm.

"And you were all discussing murder,—and how it could be done!" she cried, in an hysterical whisper that ended in a faint shriek.

"What's that?" asked Kinney, "all discussing methods of murder? When?"

"Last night," said Loft, calmly. "Mr. Curran was a Detective Story writer and we all talked of such matters to him."

"Yes, we did," Stella Lawrence said; "and each chose a different means. And last night I dreamed—"

"Now, Stella," Anna interrupted, "you will not tell your dream, I forbid it!"

"We don't care especially for dreams," the Doctor said, "we want facts. Will you each in turn please tell me, if you heard or saw anything suspicious or unusual,—after you had said good-night and gone to your rooms? You, Mr. Loft?"

"Not a thing," said Loft, promptly. "I closed my bedroom door, and heard nothing at all till morning."

Ned Knox and Angel Bob Baldwin said the same thing, and declared they had heard nothing whatever.

But Mr. Meredith was more informative.

"I did," he asserted; "I heard footsteps in the hall several times after I had retired."

"You were wakeful?" asked Kinney.

"I'm a poor sleeper always. Mrs. Meredith slept soundly, and was not disturbed, but I heard a stealthy tread passing my door, and thinking it might be some one desiring me I opened my door and looked out."

"Whom did you see?"

"I don't know who it was, but I saw someone just disappearing into Mr. Curran's room, and the door closed at once."

"You are sure it wasn't Mr. Curran himself?"

"I think not, because I heard voices talking. Of course I could make out no words, of course I didn't try to do so, but it was either Mr. Curran or a visitor of his who went in at that door."

"The hall was dark?"

"Dimly lighted by a low light at the farther end. It was fairly dark at our end."

"And this man that you saw—"

"Pardon me, sir," Mr. Meredith's voice was apologetic, "I didn't say it was a man."

"Was it not?"

"I don't think so."

"Ah; could it have been a chambermaid, with fresh towels?"

"It might have been."

"You know it was a woman?"

"It was a person wearing a long, dark shawl or cape, as if to conceal the figure. As I say, it was dark, and I could not see her clearly, but,—yes, if I am asked, I must say it was quite evidently a woman."

"You did not recognize her identity?"

"I did not. As soon as I saw the matter in no way concerned me, I closed my door and went back to bed."

"You heard nothing further?"

"Perhaps half an hour later I heard Mr. Curran's door open again."

"And the lady came out?"

"I don't know. I didn't open my own door that time. It was none of my affair."

"At what time was this, Mr. Meredith?"

"This last time was shortly after half-past two."

"How do you know?"

"The clock in the upper hall strikes the half hours. In my wakefulness I had heard it strike half-past one, and two o'clock, and this time it struck half-past two. It was a few moments later that I heard Mr. Curran's door open and shut for the second time."

"And you didn't look out into the hall?"

"No."

"Did you hear anything?"

"I heard light footsteps,—so light as to be scarcely audible."

"Passing your door?"

"Yes; going along the hall."

"Then you heard any other door open or shut?"

"I did not,—though I listened for it."

"And you have no idea who the woman was?"

"Not the slightest."

"Was she tall or short?"

"Neither, especially. I saw only the dim figure, apparently a woman, with a long shawl or robe that concealed the outlines of her figure."

"Did she wear anything on her head?"

"I couldn't notice anything. The light was too faint to discern that."

"It must have been a housekeeper or maid taking some forgotten necessaries to his room," said Loft, decidedly. "There is no other explanation."

"You can't make a suspect out of that woman, anyway," put in Roly Mears. "For, you see, whoever it was, Mr. Curran locked his door after her departure."

"If Mr. Curran was murdered, he couldn't have locked his door after the murderer," said Detective Kinney, curtly.

"Nor could the murderer have locked it after himself," said Bob. "That's a hard nut, Mr. Kinney. How are you going to crack it?"

"I'm not taking the case by that handle," Kinney said, with a dogged expression. "I start first with an investigation of the whereabouts and doings of everyone in the house; next, I look for a motive—"

"That's a sorry quest," Loft said; "no one in this house could have possibly had a motive for murdering Hugh Curran. There's an absolute fact to start with."

"Nothing of the sort," snapped the Countess. "You don't know, Valentine, that some of your servants hadn't a previous acquaintance with that man,—and, maybe, had some old grudge to pay off,—something serious enough to call forth such revenge as murder. I had small use for Mr. Curran myself."

"Tut, tut; Countess," began Roly Mears, but she interrupted him:

"Don't you tut tut me! I merely say such a thing is possible, and Valentine has no right to say it isn't."

"As a matter of fact," Loft returned, "I wasn't thinking of the servants. It is possible in their case, I suppose. But I meant that all of us, never having met Hugh Curran before, surely had no motive for murdering him."

"I've met him before," said Angel, "but only in the relation of client and book dealer,—and our transactions were always most amicable and satisfactory."

"Don't be silly!" and Loft began to lose patience. "I meant and I repeat it, Mr. Kinney, neither I, myself, nor any of my guests have had sufficient social acquaintance with Mr. Curran to have felt enmity toward him or to have any motive for killing him. I trust you will find out who did it,—if it is a murder; I trust you will prove it a suicide if it is one; but in any case, I hope you will be able to remove the body shortly, and to finish up this inquiry as soon as may be, and leave us to ourselves."

"I should be glad to do all that, Mr. Loft," the detective said looking serious, "but these things are not so easily disposed of. It is my duty to investigate thoroughly, and my duty must be done. These inquiries are necessary as a preliminary measure, and then I shall proceed to the real work of investigation. Mrs. Knox, I learn that the rooms occupied by you and your husband are near Mr. Curran's room also,—did you see or hear this woman Mr. Meredith tells of?"

"No, I didn't," replied Anna, haughtily, "and he didn't either. Mr. Meredith dreamed that or imagined it. Who in the world would be trailing into Mr. Curran's room at that hour? Maids don't take towels to guests after midnight,—had Mr. Curran wanted any service, the butler would have looked after him. None of the ladies of our house party visited Mr. Curran in his room and so I say Mr. Meredith dreamed or imagined that whole yarn!"

"That's right, Anna," and the Countess nodded her head, emphatically. "If any one did go there, it must have been Mrs. Meredith—"

"Madam!" interrupted Mrs. Meredith's husband.

"Why not?" asked the Countess, coolly. "She might have heard the poor man having a stroke or an illness, and thought she could be of help. Mrs. Meredith is, of course, of an age when such a kind act would not be unfitting."

"I can assure you, Mrs. Meredith did nothing of the sort. I resent your implication that she might have done so!"

"But, Mr. Meredith," Anna's tone was velvety though her eyes glittered, "you laid us all open to that same implication. You declared that some one of us went into Mr. Curran's room."

"I am not considering the manners or morals of this party," Doctor Gilvray said, severely. "As County Medical Examiner, it is my place to learn all I can regarding this affair. I wish you all to speak as frankly as Mr. Meredith has done—"

"Whether it's true or not?" said Anna, flippantly.

"I want only the truth. Mrs. Knox, from your brief acquaintance with Mr. Curran, would you say he was a man on the verge of committing suicide?"

"Most certainly not," said Anna, promptly. "He had too many irons in the fire. He was too deeply in love with life. His new book will be published next week. His recent book, made into a Moving Picture, will be released shortly, and he looked forward with eagerness to seeing it on the films. No, sir, last night, that man had no more intention of committing suicide than I have this minute!"

"You liked him, Mrs. Knox?"

"Very much," said Anna, heartily. "He was entertaining, witty, courteous,—and, a trifle flirtatious."

"Ah, a fine line of virtues. You learned a great deal of him in one evening."

"Yes, I did. We went for a long walk, and he told me a lot about himself."

"He did! Then perhaps you can tell us of his life,—his home."

"He had no home,—I mean no house. He lived at hotels or clubs, rather a roamer, I gathered,—going from one city to another as the whim took him."

"He was married?"

"He had been. He was divorced."

"Recently?"

"About six years ago, I think he said."

"Do you know whom he married?"

"He did not mention her name to me. I suppose it could be easily learned."

"I daresay. Did he mention the cause of his divorce?"

"He did not. We merely touched on the subject. I had no curiosity concerning the lady. He was simply an amusing companion for an evening. That's all I know of Mr. Hugh Curran."

"And you know nothing more of him, Mr. Knox?"

"Nothing whatever, and I wish I knew less! I did not like him at all. I thought him egoistical and unduly familiar."

"Oh, come, now, Ned," Angel put in; "don't show off your asinine jealousy just now. Curran was all right,—an all-round good sort. We all know why you don't cotton to him, but don't lug it into your testimony."

"I have no testimony to give," Knox said, sullenly. "I know nothing at all of the matter, and I want to know nothing. I hope, with Mr. Loft, you will arrange to remove the remains as soon as you can do so."

"That will be attended to as quickly as possible," Doctor Gilvray assured him, and the sapient Examiner smiled to himself at this exhibition of marital jealousy.

But indeed, Anna not infrequently gave her faithful and devoted husband a bad quarter of an hour because of her various coquetries.

CHAPTER 5

ROLY TAKES THE LEAD

IT was a wearisome grilling, and it got them nowhere.

Detective Kinney was logical and consequent in his questionings and Doctor Gilvray was keen and shrewd in his comments and deductions, but when it was over nobody seemed to know anything save that Hugh Curran was dead.

Some held the opinion that he had committed suicide, others that he was murdered, but most of the listeners to the scanty evidence were utterly at sea as to any satisfactory conclusion.

"It is the old problem, after all," said Roly Mears, his round, jolly face unusually grave. "An inexplicable death in an unenterable room. What's the answer?"

"Ned," Loft said, suddenly, "you said these Sealed Room detective stories bored you to death because they were so easy of solution."

"No, Val, I didn't quite say that. I said they bored me because I'd read so many, and the solution was rarely a satisfying one. However, here's a real problem of that sort right under our noses. It'll be queer if we can't, some of us, dope it out."

"I say so, too," cried Roly. "Let's do the detective work ourselves,—under Mr. Kinney's supervision, of course."

He added the last phrase because of a somewhat indignant expression on the detective's face.

"I'll tell you what," said Angel, "let's organize a detective squad of our own,—us four, you know,—Val, Ned, Roly and myself, and work independently of Mr. Kinney, but reporting to him any findings or conclusions that we consider worth while."

Kinney looked rather patronizing, but nodded his head indulgently. "I'll be glad of any help," he said, sincerely, but didn't add his secret thought, which was that precious little help was likely to reach him from the quartette of amateur detectives.

"And remember this," said the Countess, in her acid way, "you men were all discussing the ease and grace of certain methods of assassination,—suppose one of you should turn out to be the criminal."

"Such jesting is very ill-timed, Countess," Anna flared out, "you ought to be ashamed of yourself."

"Perhaps she isn't jesting," said Pauline, slowly.

"Then she ought to be even more ashamed of herself!" Anna declared. "Anyway, I'm going to help in this detective business,—I've the instinct, or whatever you call it, myself. I can deduce,—and all that."

"So can I," said Stella. "And I have psychic powers—"

"We don't want those," said Knox. "Deliver me from spook messages about a mystery. They only make matters worse."

"I want nothing to do with it," Pauline said, decidedly. "And I wish you men wouldn't take it up. You'll only get notoriety and horrid publicity without accomplishing anything. What can you do, more than professional detectives can?"

"Oh, lots," Roly Mears assured her. "Why, it's a chance of a lifetime. You see, while we're all sorry for the poor chap, yet it isn't the grief we would feel for a more personal friend,—and, so, we're free to follow up clues and evidences, no matter where they lead. Now, here's my platform. The death of Hugh Curran was not a natural death, nor an accidental one, either. The doctor vouches for that. The man was either killed by another or he killed himself. To my mind, the suicide theory is out of the question, for the simple reason that no container of the poison can be found."

"Has been found," corrected Angel. "Perhaps it will yet be discovered."

"We haven't searched Curran's room yet," said Roly. "I mean searched it carefully,—for clues, you know."

"Then let's do it now," proposed Knox. "If Doctor Gilvray wants to question us more, later, we'll all be here. I've no intention of leaving."

"I'd like very much to go," said Mr. Meredith, mildly. "These unfortunate circumstances are trying to my wife's nerves, and, I admit, also to my own. If nobody objects, we'd like to leave on the afternoon train."

"I want you all to do exactly as you please, in that matter," Loft said, courteously. "Unless the authorities wish to hold anybody, let each one feel free to carry out his or her own wishes. Pauline, dear, do you want to go?"

Pauline's face was a study. She looked pitifully at Loft, and seeing his own evident anxiety regarding her decision, she said, after a moment's pause; "I'll stay, please. I know, Valentine, you'll have lots of bothers and responsibilities, and perhaps I can share them,—or help you in some way."

"You'll help me just by your presence," he assured her, and his smile of relief told her how glad he was at her decision to stay.

"I shall stay," declared the Countess. "It all interests me exceedingly, and I want to see how the case works out."

"I want to go," Anna said, "and I want to go quick. Ned, can't we get off this afternoon, when the Merediths go?"

"I think not," said Knox, with so positive an air that Anna began to pout. She well knew that when her husband's face assumed that look of absolute finality, all her pleas and prayers were of no avail.

Almost always she wound her easy-going husband round her finger, but when he was determined on any subject, it was not in her power to move him.

"Moreover, Anna," the Countess said, "I doubt if any of these men would be allowed to leave the place until the mystery is cleared up. You seem to forget that if Mr. Curran was murdered, it must have been by someone in the house—"

"Nonsense, Countess!" Loft exclaimed, "if you talk like that, I'll send you away."

"Perhaps the Countess herself is the criminal," said Anna, spitefully. "For all we know, she has known Mr. Curran before. And the veiled woman that Mr. Meredith saw has yet to be identified."

"I didn't say veiled," Mr. Meredith put in, mildly.

"Well, shawled, scarfed,—whatever she was," Anna cried. "Anyway, she must be named, before we can go much further."

"We!" said her husband. "Are you too helping in the detective work?"

"If you are, Ned. I will take it on myself to hunt out that woman, if you like."

"Oh, Anna," said Pauline, greatly distressed, "don't mix up in these awful matters. It's bad enough to have the men do it, but let us women keep out of it!"

"I shan't keep out of it," said Stella, decidedly. "I shall stay, of course, and I know I can help some. You'll all be glad of my assistance before you're through."

"Perhaps you can dream who that woman was," Anna suggested.

"Perhaps I can," and Stella looked or tried to look mystical. "I can sometimes summon dreams that are revelations."

"Never mind that part of it," said Mears, impatiently. "It seems you're all going to stay except the Merediths. But you women must keep out of the actual investigations. If I take the lead in this thing—"

"Who asked you to?" cried Angel.

"Since I am taking the lead in this thing," Mears went on, "I propose that we first go and take a look at the room. I'm sure that we must find among Curran's belongings some hint or clue to the whole matter."

"It's a little unusual to have a band of amateur detectives working with the officers of the law," said Doctor Gilvray, slowly, "but in this very strange case, I'm not sure but it's a good thing. You men are shrewd and keen,—you may discover some important evidence. I hope, Kinney, you will raise no objections."

"Not a bit, sir. I'm quite ready to accept any help they can give me. But I must reserve the right to pass on their findings, whether material evidence or deductions."

"All right, old top," Mears said, "we agree to that. It's much better to work in harmony than to be pitted against you."

The body of Hugh Curran had been removed to the establishment of the local undertaker, and an autopsy had been held.

The final report of this was brought to Doctor Gilvray, and he read it to himself before announcing its contents.

"It's a bit strange," he said at last. "The death of Mr. Curran was positively due to hydrocyanic acid,—which, as you doubtless know, is Prussic acid,—a deadly poison. This was administered through the mouth, as the odor was distinct and unmistakable. But no traces are found in the stomach."

"Yet the poison must have been swallowed to produce death?" said Knox interrogatively.

"Probably,—yet not quite necessarily. However, I can't conceive of a circumstance which would imply the poison in his mouth and not in his stomach, unless he ejected it at once. And there is no evidence of that."

"Look here, doctor," Mears said; "reconstruct the case. I hold suicide impossible, because that poison must have been a powder, in a paper, or, a liquid, in a vial. Isn't that true?"

"Yes," said Gilvray, briefly.

"Then as we find no paper and no vial, it must have been administered by someone else. It must have been done purposely. Therefore it was murder. There is no alternative. As to how the murderer left the room locked behind him,—that is the problem we must solve. And no matter how difficult, it will be easier than to prove a suicide with no container to be found."

"Sounds plausible, Roly," Angel said, his blue eyes staring into vacancy, as they always did when his imagination was working. "But you've neglected one theory. Suppose Curran did take the poison himself, and suppose there was someone in his room later, who removed the bottle or the paper."

"Why would he?" said Mears, thinking hard.

"I don't know, I'm sure. Only, if a murderer could get out, leaving the door locked behind him, so could a man who was not the murderer."

"That's surely true, Angel, but I can't see any reason for it."

"We can't see any reason for the murder,—or the suicide, or whatever it is," Loft said; "But, to my mind, we can investigate just the same before we know which it is,—and so perhaps discover which it is. Though, first of all, I think we must find out about Curran's people."

"You don't have to do that, Val; the police are taking charge of it all." It was Pauline who spoke, and her voice was infinitely gentle, as if glad to relieve Loft of any responsibilities.

"Yes," Kinney told them, "we are making wide inquiries. We've sent a man down to New York to look through Curran's rooms at the hotel where he lived."

"What about the Country Club up here?" Knox asked. "Is he a member, or who put him up?"

"No, he wasn't a member," Kinney said; "and he had letters from John Bingham and Augustus Hedden,—each putting him up for two weeks. It's all right that way, but Mr. Bingham and Mr. Hedden are both in Europe, and we can't get in touch with them immediately. However, we've no reason to think of Mr. Curran other than as a first class and right minded gentleman. I've sent another officer to his publishers in New York. We'll soon learn all about Mr. Curran's circumstances and relatives. And of course that knowledge may give us a line on the criminal. But, so far, we've not the ghost of a suspicion of the motive behind the crime."

"That's what makes it interesting," insisted Mears. "And there are queer things about it. For instance, where's Curran's watch?"

"Did he have one?" asked Doctor Gilvray. "There was none on his watch fob when I looked him over."

"He had one on last night," Stella informed them. "I saw him take it out and look at it twice during the evening."

"So did I," said Bob. "It was a very thin gold one, on a fob. He had it in his trousers pocket."

"Yes, I noticed it," the Countess offered. "I saw him open it, too. There was a picture in the case,—a woman."

"Could you see it?" asked Angel.

"Not to recognize it," the Countess replied. "I only caught a glimpse of a woman's face."

"And that watch is gone?" cried Kinney. "Then that's a clue in itself! The woman took it!"

"What woman?"

"The one Mr. Meredith saw going into Curran's room."

"And she killed him?" asked Stella, her eyes large and bright with interest.

"Now, look here," said Mears, "you're going too fast. That watch may be in his room. He may have taken it from his pocket—"

"Then he left the fob in its place," said the doctor. "For I took his valuables myself, and gave them over to Kinney. There was a fob, and three pearl studs and a collar button,—real gold,—and cuff-links."

"Anything else in his pockets?" asked Loft.

"Only a couple of handkerchiefs and a bunch of keys,—a very small bunch. Oh, yes, a short lead pencil, and a card or two,—of no evidential importance."

"Evidential importance is a serious thing," said Mears, didactically. "You can't always recognize it at first. Come on, I'm impatient to examine that room. Now, Kinney you may come, and we four men,—that's all. You women cannot!"

This last was emphatic, because Anna and the Countess had risen quickly from their chairs with every indication of joining the party.

Anna pouted and the Countess stormed, but to no avail. They were not allowed to have their way, and the five men went off together.

The room had not been disturbed in any way. Save for the absence of the still, stark body they had seen in the easy chair, everything was the same as they had seen it at the time of the forced entrance.

"Don't touch things, boys," begged Mears. "Let's work together and systematically. First, we know Curran had not begun to prepare for bed. He had apparently sat down in his chair for a time. He had not smoked, though."

"Why, Roly, see the cigar ashes on the floor!" and Loft pointed down.

"Those he scattered before dinner," said Mears, imperturbably. "You see, the ash trays on the table at his side are clean and empty. I know the chambermaid cleans those when she turns down the bed, I can tell from my own room. And there are no burnt matches, no stubs of cigars or cigarettes. So, I know those few ashes on the floor were strewn there in the afternoon. Curran was an untidy sort, and I daresay the maid wasn't overparticular,—or, she failed to notice the ashes. Anyway, I am sure he didn't smoke after he came to his room last night. What did he smoke?"

This was all self-evident, for had he smoked there must have been a stub or a match in evidence.

Kinney looked at Mears with growing respect, and awaited his next words.

"Now, there's that little basket of nuts." Roly stared hard at a small filigree silver basket on the table. It was half full of salted almonds. "Where did that come from?"

"That was on the dinner table," Loft said, promptly. "I suppose after dinner, it was on the sideboard,—Binns would put it there,—and perhaps Curran was fond of nuts and brought it upstairs with him."

"Wrong," said Angel, looking a little amused. "I brought it up to him. As we all started upstairs, I asked Curran if he wanted anything. And he said, 'I'm ravenous for some of those salted nuts we had at dinner.' So I went to the dining room, corralled the basket and brought it up here to him."

"Then you were in this room with him?" said Kinney.

"Yes, stayed fifteen or twenty minutes. He got started on old books, and he would have talked on forever, but I was sleepy, so I told him I'd discuss the things in the morning."

"Describe the whole interview," said Kinney, briefly.

"All right," said Angel. "I brought up the nuts, tapped at the door, and Curran said, 'Come in.' So I came in, and Curran closed the door after me."

"Why did he do that?"

"I thought it queer myself at first, but he wanted to ask me to get him a special book, and the details were rather a private matter."

"Of course," Mears said. "Go on, Angel, did he like the nuts?"

"Yes, he thanked me, and began eating them. But rather absent-mindedly,—as to the nuts, I mean,—for he was deeply interested in the book he wanted me to get for him."

"What was the book?" asked Kinney.

"It is a rare old book,—a Caxton, dated 1485. It is called 'A Book of the Noble History of King Arthur.' Here is the catalogue, you may see the item."

Baldwin picked up a bookdealer's catalogue from the table, and opened it at a turned down and well-thumbed page. The item was as he had stated it.

"Woodcuts!" exclaimed Loft, his eyes glistening at the description. "I say, Angel, get it for me, will you?"

"If you like," said Baldwin, "and if you want to pay for it. It's worth a mint of money."

"Well, I'll have to think it over. Go on with your story."

"That's about all," said Baldwin. "We talked over the book, Mr. Curran was most desirous to have it, and I promised to do the best I could about the price. Then, though he asked me to stay and have a smoke, I didn't care about it, and I left him and went to my room."

"Did he seem in any way excited or nervous?" Kinney inquired.

"Not a bit nervous. A little excited about the book. Collectors are always excited over an important purchase."

"And you left him sitting in that chair?"

"I left him sitting almost exactly as he was found this morning. When I went out the door, I said 'don't rise,' and he didn't. I closed the door behind me. He must have risen later, to lock it, but, apparently he returned to the same seat,—even the same posture. I have no doubt he pored over the book catalogue again."

"At what time was all this, Mr. Baldwin?" the detective asked.

"Let me see; we came upstairs shortly after midnight. About twelve-fifteen, wasn't it, Val?"

"About that."

"And I daresay I was in here with Curran half an hour, or less. I left him, I judge at about twenty minutes or quarter before one."

"Was he then wearing his watch?"

"I've no idea. If so, he didn't look at it while I was with him."

"He sure was an untidy person," said Mears, glancing about the floor.

It was strewed with Curran's belongings as well as with worthless trash. Parts of one or two newspapers had evidently been flung aside after reading, and were in various parts of the room. Near the desk, Curran had evidently sharpened a lead pencil, dropping the chips on the rug. Near the dresser, whose top drawer was open, two handkerchiefs, clean ones, lay on the floor, and two more on the dresser top, while those in the drawer were tossed in a rumpled heap.

"He went for a handkerchief, and tossed over the whole lot to find the one he wanted," said Kinney.

"Or to find something he had hidden under the heap," Mears suggested. The detective stared at him.

"You're uncanny," he said; "you're doubtless right! Why would he go for a clean handkerchief with two in his pockets?"

"Why, Roly, you're the real thing in sleuths!" Knox exclaimed. "Go to it, boy! We'll get at the truth yet!"

"Will you help, Ned?"

"Of course, all I can. What next, Roly?"

"Well, here are all these torn papers on the floor near the chair he sat in. I doubt if they mean much, even if we could piece them together, for he wouldn't throw around anything of a private nature. However, I'll piece 'em out, and see. Hello, among them is a toothpick paper,—a printed one. Oh, it's one of the Country Club ones. Probably had it in his pocket."

"No, he didn't, smarty!" and Angel smiled at Roly's earnest face. "I gave it to him. The man had a predilection for toothpicks,—asked Binns for one after dinner. Poor Binns nearly threw a fit, but he dug up a wooden one. So, knowing Curran's weakness, I offered him a first-class sealed-paper Club quill, and he was as pleased as could be. Here's the toothpick itself, on the table."

Angel picked it up, gingerly, looked at it as if it might be evidence, and said, "Sherlock Holmes would construct a whole man from this."

"We don't want to construct a man from that," Mears scoffed. "We want the criminal. Throw that away, Angel, it means nothing."

Baldwin went over to the waste basket and even as the toothpick dropped from his fingers said, "There's a lot of things in the basket,—better give 'em the once over, Roly."

"They'll keep. Mostly book catalogues and wrappings off of things. I glanced at 'em. Well, we're not getting much of anywhere, are we? Guess I'll piece out these torn papers, and see what comes of it."

"I see Jackson coming," announced Kinney, from the window, "he'll have news from the Club people. Let's go down and see him."

CHAPTER 6

WHAT TESSIE SAW

AS the others started for the door, Ned Knox touched Mears on the arm and detained him.

"Look here, Roly," he said, "we can't handle this thing with gloves on, you know."

"Meaning?"

"That we must look where evidence points,—even if it's to one of ourselves."

"You or me?"

"No, I don't mean that,—but,—oh, well, there's no use mincing matters. Wasn't Angel the last one known to have seen Curran alive?"

"There's the visiting lady—"

"I don't believe there was one. Old Meredith dreamed that,—or made it up."

"Why for?"

"To create a sensation—"

"Not his rôle. He's no Thrill Builder. I'm banking on that woman."

"Well, anyway, take Angel into consideration. I passed the room while he was in here and I can tell you he and Curran were quarrelling."

"Seriously?"

"Very seriously. And it was something about a needle."

"A needle?"

"Yes,—it may sound absurd, but they were discussing a needle. And may it not be that Angel introduced the poison by means of a hypodermic needle?"

"I'd laugh at your suggestion, Knox, only it does seem as if that might have been the method used. The doctors could easily have overlooked the tiny scar it would make. And, do you see, a murderer using that means, would, if clever enough, touch the poison to the dead man's lips, which would explain the odor of acid in his mouth, yet no trace in his stomach."

Mears looked at Ned Knox, thoughtfully.

"You've built up a case against Angel. Why?"

"Only because there's evidence that way,—and no other." Knox returned.

"But what motive could Angel possibly have? Curran was a profitable client,—I know myself, Bob has made a lot of money off of the books he has sold him. Why kill the goose that lays the golden eggs?"

"Never mind motive, until you get your man."

"No, Ned, never mind the man until you find the motive. However, we'll look into Master Bob's case, and see what we can discover."

"There ought to be clues in this room,—more, I mean than we've found."

"There certainly are enough 'feathers left around,'" and Roly smiled at the littered floor.

"Come on," called Kinney impatiently from the hall. "I'm waiting to lock the door."

They accompanied the detective downstairs, where Jackson waited with his report.

"I found out quite a lot about Mr. Curran," Jackson began, "yet none of it seems to amount to much. He was born in Indiana, but lived most of his later life in California. For the past two years he has been a writer, but for about six years before that, he was a Movie actor."

"Not an Adonis!" observed Mears.

"No; he played character parts. They say he was fine as an old man. Well, he gave up the Pictures for a literary life, and made an immediate hit with his detective stories. He has only been writing them two years, but he has done three or four that have come well up towards the Best Sellers line."

"What was his real name?" Kinney asked.

"The Movie People didn't seem to know,—Dyer or Dwyer, they said. But I went to his New York publishers, and they told me it was Hugh Dwyer."

"Why did he adopt another?"

"The publisher said, that as he was not sure his first book would be a success, he chose a *nom de plume*. Then, when the book proved popular, he retained the name of Curran."

"Plausible enough,—no harm in all that."

"No; then I went to one or two clubs he belonged to, and all gave him a clean record, yet no one knew much about him definitely."

"What do you mean, definitely?"

"I mean as to his ancestry, or relatives. I can't find that he has any kin whatever. Still, I've only just learned the name of Dwyer, so I may trace by that. I've been working on the Curran name."

"You'll have to wire the California people—"

"I can't find any California people. The M. P. Company he was with, failed and disbanded over a year ago, and it's next to impossible to learn any facts from Movie people anyway. They are the most elusive, evasive folks in the world. Oh, I'll track down Hugh Dwyer, but it'll take some work to do it."

"Was he a married man?"

"Divorced. I found that out, but nobody knows when or why or from whom."

"The records would show all that."

"Yes, but what records? You can't comb the whole United States."

"Well, stick to it, Jackson. Had he no chums in New York? No intimate friends at the Clubs? No women friends? And he had no servants? No man? Surely he wasn't absolutely alone!"

"He seems to have been, Mr. Kinney. He lived at the Grampian Annex and while they give him A-1 rating, they know nothing of his private life. The manager told me Mr. Curran often had ladies to dine or lunch with him, and sometimes small parties, but everything was always decorous and correct. In fact, he was just a decent man about town, who kept his own counsel and made a confidant of nobody. At least, that's all I've got so far. He was fond of the ladies, but I heard no breath of scandal or unpleasant rumor anywhere."

"Exemplary chap," said Mears. "But the hardest sort to tackle. However, it's interesting to crack a tough nut like that. I'll bet I can find out a lot about him,—and without leaving this house."

"Go ahead, Roly," Loft said; "I want to find his folks, he must have some. I feel a certain responsibility, since he died in my house. And I want somebody to shift that responsibility onto."

"I don't blame you!" said Angel. "It's a horrid situation. If no one turns up, shall you bury him, Val?"

"Have to, I suppose. Or let the Funeral Company take charge of the whole affair."

"Don't worry, Mr. Loft," said Kinney. "The Law will dictate about the obsequies and all that."

"All right," Loft said, and he sighed wearily. "And I'd be obliged if the Law would clear up the matter, and find the criminal,—if any,—and free me and my friends from this exceedingly unpleasant pall of suspicion that over-hangs the house!"

"Suspicion!" cried Knox. "Nonsense, Val, who is suspected?"

"We all are," Loft returned, "The police have got hold of that fool conversation we had about methods of murder, and the ease with which it could be committed, and they think some one of us is responsible for the taking off of Hugh Curran."

"What rubbish!" Angel spoke lightly, but Mears and Ned Knox watched him closely.

"It may be rubbish," said Kinney, stolidly, "but if there's only one way to look, we have to look that way. And who can see any way to look for a murderer outside this house?"

"But, man, the room door was locked," Mears exclaimed, still watching Bob. "How could one of us manage that?"

"The windows were fastened," Kinney retorted. "How could an outsider manage that?"

"The windows were open a little, at top and bottom," Bob said, slowly.

"Yes, sir, but only six-inch apertures, and patent catches held them immovable. I've investigated all that, and nobody could possibly have entered from outside."

"There's a balcony beneath the windows," said Loft, meditatively. "It runs all along that side of the house."

"Yes, I know," Kinney agreed, "and anybody could have walked along there. Anybody could even have shot through the six inch opening,—but no intruder could poison a man that way."

"Righto," said Mears, "I saw all that. And the bathroom window is small and high and practically inaccessible."

"Positively inaccessible," corrected Kinney. "It's twenty feet from the ground, and no window near enough to climb across from. And if anyone had used a ladder, marks would show on the white paint outside. It is entirely unmarred."

"That window's too small to crawl through, anyway," Loft said. "And, another thing, the night watchman patrols this place thoroughly. No one could go up a ladder, and remain even a few minutes, and return by the ladder without being discovered by lynx-eyed old Gideon. No, cut out all thought of an outside entrance. But that doesn't preclude an outsider,—I mean someone not of our own household. An intruder could, I daresay, have entered the house during the day, and concealed himself until the time was ripe."

"Yes, that must have been the way of it," Knox argued. "We don't know how he got in and out of Curran's room, but he did,—so there must have been some way. I think the absence of Curran's watch proves a robber."

"Why did the robber leave all the other jewelry, then?" asked Bob, but Knox had no ready reply.

"I'm going to talk with some of your servants, Mr. Loft," Kinney informed him. "I think I'll get better results that way, than by having them up here."

"I'll go with you," volunteered Angel Bob. "I want to get a line on the servants' yarns."

"Nobody else, then," decreed Kinney, as Knox rose, too. "I don't want a posse."

Bob and the detective went to the pleasant sitting room that was provided for the servants' use, and summoned the principal ones to conference. They called them singly, and after the non-committal testimony of the butler, the second man, the cook, and one or two maids, they felt disheartened and hopeless of gaining any information.

But a giddy, flippant little parlor maid gave them a hint of one stone left unturned.

"I do know sumpthing," she said, with a toss of her marvellous curly head; "but I'm not sure I ought to tell it."

"You not only ought to, but you must tell it!" Kinney said, sternly; "out with it, now!"

But this made the little minx turn stubborn, and utterly unafraid of the Arm of the Law, she made a face at the detective and pouted mutinously.

Angel laughed outright at this picture of dignity and impudence, for Kinney's dignity was so offended as to make him look like a collapsing balloon, and the girl's pretty face was roguish and stubborn, both at once.

He came to the rescue with his inimitable tact and irresistible charm.

"Now, Rose,—your name is Rose, isn't it?"

"No, sir, it's Violet."

"Prettier yet. Now, then, Violet, you're to tell all you know,—or you'll be an exceedingly sorry little Violet. Take it from me, my dear,—if you hold back this information another minute, you'll be—put in the lockup!"

Bob breathed the last three words in a menacing whisper, with a sudden change from a smiling face to a lowering, threatening countenance, and so effective was his manner that Violet jumped in sudden terror.

"Yes," Bob rubbed it in, "in the lockup,—the jail! No place for pretty little girls,—all stone walls, and bread and water, and—rats."

A shriek from the frightened Violet told of her surrender, and with a return of his suavity, Bob said: "Out with it now,—my dear. Tell the story you're holding back. Does it implicate somebody else?"

"Yes,—that's it, sir. She'll kill me!"

"Oh, no, she won't. Hurry up, Violet, the lockup yawns for you!"

"Well," she looked fearfully at both men, but started in on the tale:

"It was Tessie. She—she went out last evening—"

"Was it her evening out?"

"Oh, yes, sir. But we're ordered to be in by eleven o'clock at the latest,—ten, unless we've arranged about it beforehand. Well,—Tessie,—she—"

"Get on," said Kinney, impatiently, "Tessie overstaid her time. How late was she?"

"Oh,—she—it was after one o'clock!"

"My, my, that *is* shocking!" Bob exclaimed. "It's as much as her place is worth!"

"Indeed it is," Violet agreed.

"Get on," growled Kinney. "What did she see?"

"She was so late, she crept in under the side gate,—a slim girl can just do it,—and then she watched when Gideon was out of the way, to run into the cellar door,—the one Gideon uses, and she knew she could get in. So, while she was waiting for the old man to get around to the other side of the house, she was looking about, and up on the balcony,—outside the room Mr. Curran had, she saw two people. They were Mr. Curran and a lady."

"Who was the lady?" Kinney shot out.

"Mrs. Knox," Violet said, frightened into an immediate reply by Kinney's scowl.

Angel gave a short, low whistle.

"Violet," he said, "if you ever tell that to another soul, I'll kill you,—do you hear? Yes, I *can* do it. I didn't kill Mr. Curran, but I could kill a person if I wanted to, and so sure as you breathe that to any one, I'll kill *you!* See?"

"Yes, sir," murmured Violet, trembling. "I won't tell, if you won't tell on me!"

"That your friend was out late? No, I won't tell that."

"Think a minute, Mr. Baldwin," and Kinney looked at him patronizingly, "this isn't this girl's secret. It was Tessie who saw the lady, Tessie who told Violet of it,—and who has probably told all the rest of the servants by this time."

"Yes, I think she has," said Violet, casually.

Angel swore softly to himself. He was decidedly interested in the pretty, vixenish Anna, and of all people, he hated to have her name brought into this horrible affair.

"Of course," he said, after a pause, "Mrs. Knox had no hand in the tragedy, she knows nothing of the crime,—if there was a crime,—so, Kinney, can't we suppress this bit of gossip? I can square the servants, if you'll promise not to use the story at all."

"Can't do that, Mr. Baldwin. But, if, as you say, Mrs. Knox is not implicated in the case, it can do her no great harm to have it known that she strolled on the balcony in the moonlight at one o'clock. That's not a very late hour."

"N-no,—but that isn't the point. I happen to know that the Knoxes went to their rooms shortly after twelve. If Mrs. Knox left her room again,—oh, pshaw,—let's forget it."

"I see; if she left her room again,—it was without the knowledge of her husband,—they had separate rooms?"

"Yes," said Bob, sullenly.

"Adjoining?"

"Bath between."

"Oh, ho! So, the lady could leave,—her room gives onto the balcony?"

"I won't tell you any more. You're building up a scandal out of what you said yourself was merely an innocent moonlight stroll. I refuse to help you drag a lovely lady into this unpleasant affair."

"Oh, I don't need your help. Run along, Violet, you've done your duty. Always tell all you know, when the Law demands it. Run away, now."

Violet went away, and her attitude was rather that of an important witness, than of one who had testified against her will.

Without another word to the furious Angel, Kinney went in search of Tessie. With a few decisive commands, in the name of the Law, he reduced her to a state of abject obedience.

She told the story, much as Violet had related it, but she went into a mass of elaborate detail,—so elaborate, that Kinney suspected a vivid imagination, in good working order.

"Yes, sir," Tessie said, rolling her eyes, as if enjoying her part, "yes, sir, it was Mrs. Knox,—I know her well. She had on a bee-yooutiful gown,—dressing-gown,—what they call negglegy, you know."

"You could discern that?"

"Oh, yes, I could see the lace ruffles, and the teeny-weeny rosebuds on it. All ribbony, and chiffony and floaty about."

Tessie's expressive hands waved in illustration of floating draperies, and so realistic was she, that Kinney felt she must have seen what she described.

"They walked up and down the balcony?"

"No,—that is they did for a minute, then they sat on the balcony rail and looked at the moon. They sat mighty close together, too."

Again the rolling eyes betokened a deep interest and appreciation. Clearly, Tessie was romantic by nature.

"And then?"

"Then, Gideon got out of the way, and I skittled into the house, through his area door, and hustled up to my own room. So that's all I know about those two."

Bob Baldwin went back to the library, where the men of the house were assembled.

All except Knox, who wasn't there, and his absence gave Bob an opportunity to speak of what was in his mind.

"I say, fellows," he began, "it's up to all of us to speak out frankly. I admit that when we all boasted how easy it would be to kill a man, and then when one is killed right here among us,—I admit, it looks queer for us all, and it ought to be understood that if there's anything—anything at all against any of us, it is to be spoken of and thrashed out."

"Right, Angel," Mears said, "and as a starter, I'll tell that you have been hinted at."

"By whom?" and Bob's question was serious.

"Well, since we're all to speak out in meetin',—by Ned Knox."

Angel sighed and looked grave.

"As he is the one I want to speak about, perhaps our stories will dovetail."

And then, to his friends and cronies, Valentine Loft and Roly Mears, Bob told the story of Tessie's observations, as retailed by Violet.

"I knew Anna was making a dead set for him," Loft said, moodily. "What a flirt she is! She didn't care two cents for Curran, really, he was just a new man for her wiles to work on. She is a vain little featherhead—"

"Hold, there, Loft,—I'm fond of Anna," Bob said with utter frankness. "Don't treat her rough."

"All right, Angel. But, seriously, if the maid's story is true, and why should we doubt it, then Anna did sneak out to the balcony,—probably after Ned was snoring,—and had her clandestine flirtation with Curran. Now, if Ned awoke, trailed her, and discovered them,—it would—he would kill Curran quicker'n a wink."

Kinney had entered, and heard this last statement.

The detective told the men such further details as he had learned from Tessie, which, of course, was the information that Anna was *en negligée*, and that the two miscreants sat close together on the balcony rail.

"Not hard to believe of Anna," Mears declared, "nor of Curran, either. And no harm done, except in view of later developments. But suppose Ned did do the irate husband act, how did he get that deadly poison, how did he get in and out of Curran's room, and why did he take Curran's watch?"

"I know!" cried Roly. "It was Anna's picture in the back of the watch!"

"Nonsense! Anna met Curran for the first time, last evening."

"Anna's cute enough to pretend anything." This from Loft. "That woman's a—forgive me, Angel,—but she is as sly and cunning as they come. I can't puzzle out the ways and means,—but there's that difficulty with any theory or assumption. Also, I won't even think wrong of Ned Knox, until he has a chance to speak for himself, but I do say this must be looked into."

"I think the worst against Knox," Roly put in, "is the way he tried to implicate Angel to me. He hinted at Bob's being the murderer,—because, forsooth, he heard Bob and Curran quarreling over something in Curran's room."

"That was at half-past twelve," said Bob, "and after one, Tessie saw Curran, evidently very much alive."

"But it was a good tack for Knox to take, to divert suspicion from himself," Roly said, thoughtfully.

CHAPTER 7

THE SISTER ARRIVES

"BUT you see, Pauline, darling, Ned Knox is impulsive, belligerent and pig-headed. If he found Anna out on the balcony flirting with Curran, he would kill him just as soon as he could manage it!"

"But how could he manage it?"

"Somebody managed it. You remember, when we talked about murder, Knox said shooting was his choice. But, he had no gun, so he had to resort to poison."

"Where could he get it?"

"Well, there's one way," Loft said, slowly. "Angel has an elaborate photographic outfit in my den. He has poisons there that he uses in his work—"

"Why has Bob an outfit of that sort?"

"He's an amateur photographer. He doesn't say much about it, because everybody is after him to take a photograph. And, too, he has to photograph title pages or something, in connection with his book business. In the New York Public Library, they have a whole room for the purpose of photographing pages of rare books for people who want them. Bob does this in a limited way. You know, Pauline, he is an artist in this rare book business. He's no amateur."

"All right. Then, say Ned did get poison from Bob's laboratory or whatever you call it, how'd he get it to Mr. Curran?"

"He could get to him easily enough. I suppose Curran would let him in, if he came to his room later. But, the thing is, how did he get out and leave the door locked behind him?"

Pauline looked deeply thoughtful. Her beautiful eyebrows came closer together as she concentrated on the problem. Her long, slim hands, clasped in her lap, seemed to tremble with the intensity of her mental effort.

At last, she gave a shrug, as if to throw aside a consideration, and said, "But, Val, that problem confronts every theory. Why don't you leave that until you get other data, pointing toward the murderer,—or the motive?"

"You're right, Pauline, and I'm glad to see it so clearly. Now looking at it that way, Ned had motive,—you know his insane jealousy of Anna,—also, he had opportunity,—for after two o'clock, nobody was awake or listening—"

"Except Mr. Meredith."

"Oh, old Pop Meredith doesn't count. Neither does Stella. They're both deluded by their subconscious dreams and vagaries."

"Yes, I think that, too. Well, Val, go on. Did Ned take Mr. Curran's watch?"

"Surely. It had Anna's picture in it."

"Then you think Anna knew Mr. Curran before yesterday?"

"Of course she did. Anna is a flirt, but no woman would progress so fast as to arrange a clandestine meeting with an utter stranger, the first time she saw him!"

"Yes,—that's so. And so late,—and in her boudoir gown—it was that,—I know the rosebudded affair Tessie described."

"Well, there you are. Lord knows I hate to suspect Ned Knox,—but evidence is against him. And, too, he tried to implicate Angel,—to my mind, that's against him, too."

"Yes, I suppose it is. But, Val, dear, must you—prosecute, or whatever you call it? Can't you hush it all up?"

"Don't see how we can, Pauly. But I will try to get it all over as soon as possible. If Ned is guilty,—I feel sure he'll have the decency to clear out pretty quick."

"If Ned is a—a murderer,—you can't expect him to have—decency."

"Of course you can. His sudden wild impulse, and the consequent act of crime, don't change his traits or habits. If Ned Knox proposes leaving here,—he wouldn't be allowed to go,—but it would prove to my mind his guilt—"

"Oh, Valentine, he never did it! He couldn't have done it!" and Pauline clasped her hands and shook her head in utter negation of the idea.

"What are you two talking about?" and the Countess sailed majestically toward the pair who sat in the swing on the veranda.

"About Mr. Curran's death," said Pauline, calmly. "What do you think, Countess?"

"I think Ned Knox killed him. Don't ask me how or when or which or what! I don't know! I only know that Ned was insanely jealous of Anna and he killed the man who—flirted with her."

"Too easy," Loft said. "Give a dog a bad name and hang him. But if it's a human dog, we must prove his claim to the bad name."

"Don't be too fussy, Val," the Countess said, shortly, "Ned Knox killed him, and now all you have to do is to check up the ways and means."

"Just like a woman!" said Loft. "Oh, yes, I say so and so is a murderer. Now somebody will please prove it."

"But what do you think, Val?" Pauline asked, her eyes on Loft's face. "Don't you think Ned did it?"

"No, Pauly,—frankly, no, I don't!"

"Oh, fiddle-dee-dee!" cried the Countess, "what does it matter who we think did it? The thing must be proved—proved!"

"All very well, Countess," Loft began, but he was interrupted by Binns, who announced, "Miss Dwyer is here, sir."

"What?" "Who?" and "Good Lord!" his hearers exclaimed, simultaneously, and immediately followed the butler into the house.

In a reception room they found a lady, tall, gaunt and aggressive.

At least, those were the qualifications that sprang first to Loft's notice.

The Countess observed that the visitor was distinctly Middle West as to voice and manner, and Pauline noted with shocked realization the tightfitting black taffeta, "travelling dress" the lady wore.

"I am Hetty Dwyer," the strange guest announced, rising as the others entered. "I am the sister of Hugh Dwyer,—known, perhaps to you as Hugh Curran."

"How do you do, Miss Dwyer," Loft said, at once, and most courteously, "it is good of you to come."

"Not at all," she spoke somewhat acidly, "I read of the death of my brother in the paper, and I hurried here at once."

"It is four days since Hugh Curran died," Loft said, slowly, "and, Miss Dwyer, he is now—"

"Buried?" she exclaimed, apprehensively.

"No; his body is in the receiving vault,—at the undertaker's place," he assured her. "You may see him again,—if you wish."

"Of course I wish," she cried. "My only brother. My loved Hugh. Certainly I wish to see him again, before he is laid away forever."

"Very well, you may," Loft assured her. "And now, Miss Dwyer, since you are here, I've no doubt you can tell us something that may throw light on the strange mystery of his death."

"That I'm sure I can't do," she said, with asperity.

Miss Dwyer was a tall, angular person, with prominent cheek bones, elbows and even knees, which indicated themselves inside her scant skirts. She was perhaps forty, and old looking for her age.

She had none of the graces or amenities of urban life, rather she showed the awkward, ignorant demeanor of a country-bred woman.

But she was shrewd and keen, and absolutely unabashed.

"That's why I am here," she went on, earnestly. "I want to know who killed my brother. Any idea of suicide is utterly ridiculous—"

"But, Miss Dwyer," said Kinney, who was present, "your denunciation of a theory as utterly ridiculous, doesn't make it so."

"It does in this case," she declared, calmly, "for I know my brother's circumstances and conditions,—and I know he was looking forward to a new happiness,—to a new phase of his life, that meant, to him, nothing less than bliss."

"And what was that?" Kinney asked.

"He was about to be married," she said, with all the awe and wonder in her voice that accompanies a spinster's dream of wedlock.

"Indeed," Kinney said. "He had been married before, had he not?" Miss Dwyer's face changed. It looked scornful, even infuriated.

"Yes!" she said, "he had! To an utterly worthless woman! A silly, selfish, peevish chit, who led him a dance, until—"

"Until he got rid of her?"

"Yes, well rid of her! That woman was a millstone round his neck! The happiest day of his life was when their bonds were severed."

"You knew her, then?" Kinney asked.

"I never saw her, thank heaven! But I know how unworthy of him she was! You see, the whole affair,—I mean his meeting her, their engagement, their marriage and their divorce, all occurred within a year, within eight months,—to be exact, and I was abroad for a two-year trip at the time. But as soon as I returned, and saw my brother again, I realized how fortunate he was to be released from her."

"Her name?" asked Kinney.

"I don't really know," Miss Dwyer said. "He called her Rose or Rosalie,—but I don't think that was her real name. Yet it may have been. Her surname, I never heard. When I returned, the affair was all over, a thing of the past, and I never talked to my brother about it."

"It all has no bearing on the present problem," Kinney said slowly, "unless that wife could have been implicated in his murder,—if it is a murder."

"Oh, no, I'm sure she couldn't have been. As I understood matters, she was even more glad to get freed from him than he from her. They were totally uncongenial, and each wanted separation."

"Doubtless the marriage and divorce are all on record," Kinney observed.

"Oh, yes, I suppose so," Miss Dwyer said. "But I'm sure that woman had nothing to do with it. My brother was an adorer of women, and had dozens of affairs since his divorce. But, lately, he devoted his whole life and soul to one girl,—a Miss Fitzgerald, of Chicago. And he expected to marry her soon."

"Can we get in touch with the lady?" Kinney asked.

"I don't see why not," Miss Dwyer returned. "Yet, she can't help you. I know she loved my brother,—she would have no hand in his taking off. And if she hasn't come forward in the matter, it's merely because she knows she can be of no help, and she would naturally hate the publicity."

"That's all true enough," Loft said, thoughtfully; "yet, it seems we ought to see or hear from Miss Fitzgerald."

"I should think so!" Kinney declared.

Miss Dwyer wore a hat with one stiff, black quill feather. When she spoke emphatically, as she almost always did, this feather nodded sharply and seemed to punctuate her speech.

It did so now, as she said,

"It is absurd to think that an interview with Miss Fitzgerald would be of any help in this affair. On the contrary, Miss Fitzgerald knows nothing about the awful details, and I beg of you leave the poor girl in peace. Her grief is hard enough to bear without having the agonies and distresses of a murder trial on her shoulders as well. Now, I know, that my brother's death is the work of some of you people here. You society people,—frothy, artificial, fashionable puppets, who dance as Fate pulls the strings! And, if you have a grudge or a fancied grudge against any one, you snuff out his life with no conscience or compunction."

"Miss Dwyer," Loft spoke seriously, "I can't allow that statement to stand. We are 'society people,' as you use that term, but I assure you we are not given to murdering our fellow-men, or to accepting the fact of murder, without being shocked by it, and striving to bring the criminal to justice. I am surprised that you should think otherwise."

"I do think otherwise, and your declaration does not move me. I still believe that my brother came to his end by foul play of some one whom he trusted and deemed his friend. I am here to prove or disprove my theory. Mr. Loft, shall I remain here, under your roof, or go to some inn or other stopping place?"

"I invite you to stay here, Miss Dwyer, as long as it pleases you to do so. We are working on the mystery ourselves, and you may work with us or pursue your independent search, as you choose."

Valentine Loft was a perfect host, and his courteous manner and bland speech seemed to affect Miss Dwyer pleasantly.

"Thank you," she said; "I shall be glad to remain here a few days. As you can readily understand, I am so shocked and upset by my brother's death I can scarcely pull myself together. And to be here, on the very scene of his death, is—is unnerving,—to say the least."

Valentine Loft, beneath his urbane exterior was a very sharp and keen reasoner. And as he watched his newest guest, he doubted her sincerity of grief regarding her brother's death. She was shocked,—upset,—even stunned,—but of actual grief or sorrow he saw small trace.

His conclusions were verified, when, a moment later, Miss Dwyer began to inquire about her brother's effects.

"As I am his only heir," she said, "of course I am in full possession of all he left,—in property or assets. I know little about such matters, but I do know that Hugh's book royalties and Motion Picture royalties must amount to a considerable sum,—and all of those are naturally mine."

"Naturally," agreed Kinney. "There will, I'm sure, be no trouble about all that. Now, we want to get at the motive for the murder and the identity of the murderer. Can you give us any suggestions, Miss Dwyer."

"Only what I have already said. I'm sure Hugh's death was due to some acquaintance of his who,—well, I can't help thinking it was because of some woman. My brother was capable of sudden and deep passions for a woman, and even though he was engaged to Miss Fitzgerald, that would not prevent his violent flirtation with another woman, and through that he might have been punished by some irate husband or fiancé."

The contrast between the prim, prudish old maid, and her sophisticated talk of her brother's amours amused the Countess, who laughed outright.

"You're a true woman," she said, "and though unmarried, I daresay you've had your own little affairs,—here and there."

"You mistake me, madam," Miss Dwyer sat bolt upright. "I am above and beyond all small coquetries or intrigues. I loved my brother,—but I have never loved any other man. Moreover, I do not enjoy the society of men. While, here, I will, if you please, confine my associations mostly to the women, and from them, or through them, I hope to unravel this mystery."

And so there was another sleuth added to the corps at Valhalla, and indeed, one, who by virtue of her earnest and patient work, went far toward the final solution of the mysterious death of Hugh Curran.

The Countess frankly disliked the new comer. This was not surprising, for Countess Galaski liked few people, and rarely was amiable to a woman.

So she and Miss Dwyer tacitly agreed to be enemies, and each religiously opposed the other's opinions or contradicted the other's statements.

"They're really funny," Pauline said to Val. "If the Countess should say two and two make four, Miss Dwyer would bring any number of authorities to prove it doesn't."

"Yes, they're funny," Loft agreed, "but I can't like that Miss Dwyer. One reason being, she hates me so. I believe she thinks I killed her brother."

"Oh, Val, how could she think that?"

"She can think anything,—and the police can, too. Kinney has been looking at me askance of late. And, Good Lord, Pauline, which way is there to look? Here it's five days since Hugh Curran died under my roof, and I'm no nearer a theory of his death than we were at first."

"No; but suppose, dear, that it never should be discovered, would it matter much?"

"Indeed it would, Pauline. There would always be a cloud over this place,—over this house,—this home, which I hope will be your home. I can't ask you to accept a home with a cloud over it."

"I don't mind that, dear. I'd rather the whole affair would blow over as quickly as possible,—I hate to hear about it,—to think about it—oh, Val, let's go away somewhere until it is all over."

"I wish we might, dearest, but such a thing is out of the question. No, we must face the music,—I must, anyway. But, dear heart, sometimes I think you'd better go away for a time. It is painful for you,—"

"Don't you want me here, Val? With you?"

"Oh, I do, Sweetheart! I'm thinking only of you. Pauline, suppose there should be some important disclosure soon,—some awful fact about one of our guests—"

"Anna?"

"Yes; how did you guess? But there is evidence,—of a sort,—against Anna—"

"Valentine, put it out of your mind,—at once! Anna is absolutely blameless—"

"Of the murder,—of course. But she has been—she was—indiscreet—"

"What did she do?"

On a sudden impulse, Loft told Pauline his opinion of the story Tessie had given them.

She listened attentively, and then said: "I can believe all that,—that Anna went out on the balcony and met him,—but not that she—"

"But Pauline, dear, you don't understand. The theory is that Ned surprised them out there together, and in his jealous rage, he killed Curran."

"That could be," Pauline nodded her head thoughtfully. "But I don't believe it happened. Anyway, don't bank on it,—don't follow it up, will you, Val?"

"It isn't my doing. Roly is working from that angle. He has checked up Anna's wardrobe, and has even found the negligée in question,—with floating draperies and tiny pink rosebuds."

"Pshaw, every woman has a negligée answering that description,—I have, myself."

"Is that so, Pauline? Is it a usual model? That does seem to nullify Roly's clue."

"Of course it does. And it's a silly theory, anyway. Where's Mr. Curran's watch? Why would Ned Knox take that?"

"That's just the point. Roly thinks Anna's picture was in it."

"Anna's picture! Ridiculous!"

"Why ridiculous? That is, assuming Anna knew him before."

"Nonsense! It was never Anna's picture."

"I don't see how you can be so sure."

"Why,—I saw him flash the watch open that night, after dinner."

"Did he? What for? It was not a hunting case. He didn't have to open it to see the time."

"No."

"Tell me, Pauline, what do you mean? How did you see the picture?"

"Oh, I didn't exactly see it, Val, but I did see him flash the case open and steal a look at the picture. I couldn't see whose likeness it was, but I'm sure it was not Anna's."

"Then dear, if you saw it as distinctly as that, you must have been able to distinguish the features. Was it any one you knew?"

"No, oh, no. It was—it was the face of a stranger,—a young-looking girl, with a lot of curly hair. A pretty face, but one in no way distinguished."

"You noted it closely."

"Not intentionally. It meant nothing to me. But when it was exposed to my view, though only for a few seconds, I really saw it plainly, and I remember it."

"You'd know the face if you saw it again?"

"Yes, I'm sure I should. But why so interested, Val?"

"Only that it's one of the 'feathers left around.' I want to know what it means."

"But the watch wasn't left around."

"I mean the evidence,—the clue of the missing watch, is what we have taken to calling a feather,—that is a clue."

"Oh, yes, I see. If you could find out who that woman's face was, you think it would help you in your discoveries?"

"I do think so. Although it may have been the picture of Miss Fitzgerald,—Curran's fiancée."

"Yes, that might be," Pauline agreed, but her tone was perfunctory, and her gaze faraway,—she seemed to be utterly preoccupied. "If he was so interested in that girl," she went on, "why was Ned so irate about Anna? He couldn't have thought Mr. Curran's admiration of Anna at all serious."

"Ned is a lunatic, when it comes to Anna. I've seen him flare up and go almost crazy if she so much as smiled on a man he disliked. Poor Anna."

"Don't waste your sympathy on Anna," said Pauline.

CHAPTER 8

LITTLE ANNA'S WILES

"IT'S all very well," said Roly Mears, "for you people to stick by one another, and to shield one another. But the truth of this thing has got to come out. I'm friendly enough with all you men, I'm chivalrous enough toward the women, but all the same, I'm going to dig into this matter, and I'm going to find out who killed Hugh Curran. But I'll say at the start I don't believe the murderer was you, Valentine, or Angel. More, I don't think it was Ned Knox."

"Who do you think it was?" Loft asked, a trifle disinterestedly. He didn't think much of Roly's powers as a detective and was a little bored with his talk.

"I think it was somebody we none of us know. I think he was concealed in the house somewhere, and late that night he went to Curran's room, and Curran let him in."

"Yes,—go on."

"Then, for reasons of his own he killed Curran,—poisoned him,—and made a clever getaway."

"Leaving the door locked behind him?"

"Yes, Val, leaving the door locked behind him. We know the door was locked,—we know the murderer must have left it locked behind him,—a dead man couldn't get up and lock it. So accept those facts, and then assume any explanation you please of the locking of that door. I think it could be done with some sort of an implement,—something like a skeleton key, that could turn the door key in its own lock."

"Have you ever heard of such a thing, Roly?"

"No; I'm imagining it. But far more wonderful and complicated devices are made, and I hold that such an implement is not by any means impossible."

"If that could be done," said Loft, thoughtfully, "it eliminates one phase of the mystery. If that could be done,—anybody might have done it."

"Only some one versed in the tricks and tools of burglary," corrected Mears. "Modern burglars have very up-to-date contrivances."

"It wasn't burglary."

"No, but it may have been a burglarious entrance and exit. And the motive was, of course, something connected with Curran's past or private life, of which we know nothing. That's why, Val, I'm so keen to find out the truth. It isn't so much to avenge the poor chap's death, as to clear all of us from suspicion. The police are sure that one of our crowd did it. Ned, for choice. But they hold that after that fool conversation you chaps put up, they must find the murderer among you three. You may as well know how positive they are about this. They don't say much to you, but they do to me. And that Kinney is the most persistent person. He has a dogged stick-to-it-iveness that nothing seems to dismay. He's going to interview Anna today and ask her straight out about that balcony business."

"I wish him joy," Loft said, smiling. "He'll not get much out of Little Anna!"

But in this Loft was mistaken. At that very moment Detective Kinney was interviewing Anna Knox, and was getting a whole lot of information.

She had received him in her own boudoir, and with an eye to the setting of the stage, she was arrayed in a most fetching tea gown and was ensconced among a pile of soft pillows in the corner of a great divan.

She had chosen her rôle of confidential innocence, and her first words disarmed Kinney and roused all his sympathy.

"I'm so glad to see you," she cooed, raising sad, pathetic eyes to his stern accusing countenance. "I'm sure you can help me,—and I've no one else to look to for assistance."

The blue eyes were so trustful, the rose pink cheeks so soft, and the red mouth so appealing that Kinney did what many better and wiser men had done before him, fell for Little Anna utterly.

From that moment he was her abject slave, he could no more have accused her,—even suspected her, than he could have his own mother.

This was in no way his fault,—Nature had given him a susceptible heart, especially toward a trusting woman, and when Anna's exquisite beauty added its charm and her clever brain prompted the way, the man was entirely defenseless and simply surrendered.

But Kinney didn't know this. It was part of Anna's spell that she made her victims think they were still masters of themselves when they were abjectly under her thumb.

"Yes," she went on, her voice hopeless, her eyes despairing. "I am in a peculiar position. I can't ask my husband to help me, for he is—oh, well," she dimpled into a fleeting smile, "he is a monster of jealousy,—and you are man of the world enough to know what that means, Mr. Kinney!"

This subtle compliment further subjugated her hearer, and he bridled a little as he said, sympathetically, "Yes, yes, indeed, Mrs. Knox, I know."

"Now, to get right at the matter, Mr. Kinney, you ask me questions and I'll answer them."

Anna cuddled among her cushions, looking like a pretty child about to play an amusing game. And indeed, that was not far from her mental attitude.

Kinney pulled himself together. He must be stern, that he knew. He was dimly subconscious of the situation, and had an uneasy feeling that he was not quite in command of himself. This nerved him to strenuous effort, and he said, severely:

"Then, Mrs. Knox, is the story the maid, Tessie, tells a true one? Were you with Mr. Curran on his balcony after one o'clock that night,—the night he died?"

"It isn't his balcony," and Anna pouted prettily. "It's just as much my balcony,—both our rooms are on it."

"Yes,—I know. And you were out on your balcony—"

"Yes, I was," in a burst of frankness, "I was. The moonlight was so divine, and I could not sleep, so I slipped on a boudoir gown and stepped out to look at the lovely scene."

"And then?"

"And then, Mr. Curran chanced to step out of his window, too,—and, as was most natural, we spoke of the beauty of the night."

"Of course," said Kinney, and gazing at Anna's face, he imagined Hugh Curran noting other beauty beside that of the night.

"And you sat by him on the balcony rail?"

"Why, yes, Mr. Kinney,—I did for a moment. Now, I'll own up to you, that Mr. Curran was a fascinating man,—and that I—" she peeped at him from beneath her long lashes, "that I am—at least, I'm called a bit of a flirt— oh, well, I confess—but there was no crime in that,—was there?" The blue eyes appealed; "no real wrong in a tiny flirtation? That isn't what you detectives want to discover, is it?"

"No, no, indeed, ma'am. No, certainly not!"

"Then you don't need to say anything about it, do you? You don't need to blazon abroad my little teeny-weeny indiscretion?"

"No, no,—that isn't necessary—"

"Oh, you good Mr. Kinney! Oh, you dear man! And you promise not to say anything about it, don't you?"

"But—but it is already known. Tessie—"

"But if you and I deny it, Tessie's story won't be believed. If you'll say that I denied being out there, and that you believe my denial, no one can consider the maid's story at all. It will be entirely discredited."

"I don't see how I can do that—" Kinney looked at her perplexedly. "You see—"

"I don't see anything!" Anna playfully put both hands over her eyes, "and you don't either,"—she transferred the soft fingers to Kinney's eyes, "and so, let's forget it all."

The touch of her roseleaf hands set the man's pulses beating, and as the fingertips left his eyes, and he saw Anna's roguish, smiling face, not far from his own, he would have promised her anything she asked.

"I don't know as it's important evidence—" he began, heavily.

"It isn't evidence at all!" she cried, gaily. "I mean no evidence for or against your old murder case. Now, you know it isn't, Mr. Kinney, and you know you're going to ignore it all, and you're going to leave poor little me out of the question, and then I'll be happy and contented. And I'll owe my happiness to you,—you dear man!"

She seized his hand in both her own, and dropped a fluttering kiss on the big red paw.

This sealed Kinney's doom, and in a sort of trance, he murmured:

"What shall I tell them?"

"Tell them," Anna directed, "that you interviewed me, and that I convinced you that I was not out on the balcony at all that night. That Tessie either made up the story or that she was mistaken. That the whole matter is of no importance anyway, and that you have other and more indicative knowledge to work on."

"Yes. And what is that knowledge?"

"He's eating out of my hand," thought Anna, jubilantly.

"It's just this," she replied, gravely. "While we sat on the balcony rail,— you see, I accept you as a sharer of my secrets,—there came a knock at Mr. Curran's door. Only a light, almost timid tap, but in the silence of the night we heard it distinctly. Of course, he had to go and answer it, so he returned to his room, and I hastened to mine."

"But you lingered," the detective instinct was still at work, "you tarried long enough to peep and see who it was?"

"Oh, you wonderful man! How did you guess that?"

"Who was it?"

"I couldn't see,—but I'm sure it was a woman."

"Ah, the shawled woman of Mr. Meredith's story."

"Yes, exactly. I couldn't corroborate him, for I didn't want any one to know I was there. But since you know, and since you're going to keep it secret,—I trust you, Mr. Kinney—I feel sure you can trace that woman."

"Then I'll work on that clue, using only Mr. Meredith's statement and not telling that it is backed up by yours."

"Yes, that's just what I mean. You see, as I heard that tap, and saw Mr. Curran open the door to somebody,—that lets me out regarding—oh, I mean—you can't think me the murderess."

A glance at the baby face was enough to make any such supposition ridiculous, but Kinney was still rational enough to realize that if Anna's story of the tap at the door was a true tale, then she could have had no hand in the murder herself. And as the time coincided with the time Mr. Meredith had mentioned, he felt he had no reason to disbelieve what Anna Knox told him.

Kinney went downstairs a gladder and a wiser man. He had eliminated one possible suspect, which was one step in the right direction.

He found Loft and Angel in the library, discussing old books with Miss Dwyer.

It seemed, Valentine had offered to buy some of Hugh Curran's books from his sister, whose property they now were.

And this had roused Miss Dwyer's easily inflammable suspicions.

"That's the key to this whole mystery," she was exclaiming, as Kinney entered. "There's the motive! You two, Mr. Loft and Mr. Baldwin envied my brother some of his rarities. I've heard how wicked and greedy all collectors are! How they resort to any means to acquire a volume they have set their hearts on. I've been told how they will lie, cheat, steal, yes, even murder to get a choice specimen. My brother had a wonderful collection,—I know something of these matters myself. I know his Black Letter books are among the finest known. I know he had certain volumes that all the collectors in the country were trying to get away from him. I know that only a connoisseur in these things would know the value of his possessions, and would go to any lengths to get them. Mr. Kinney," she turned to the detective, "there is your motive,—my brother was killed because he owned a valuable library. Now, you find his murderer!"

Attracted by the loud voice of Miss Dwyer, Stella, who was passing, came in.

"I couldn't help overhearing," she said. "And, too,—though I know Val, you don't take any interest in dreams,—yet I want to tell you of the vision I had last night."

"Nonsense," Loft began, "but Kinney stopped him."

"Let her tell it, Mr. Loft," he counselled. "Though only a dream it may be of benefit,—there may be a hint in it."

"It was so vivid a dream," Stella said, "that I call it a vision. I saw a large library,—a room full of books,—it may have been a book shop, but the shelves were filled with old worn volumes. There were four men present, but all wore cowls,—such as monks wear. I could see none of their faces. But one seemed to be the owner of the books, and the others were visitors. There was much handling and discussion of the volumes. There also seemed to be quarrelling or ill feeling among the men. Of only two books could I discern the titles."

"What were they?" asked Kinney, as Stella paused.

"One was '*Rosalie*,'—and one was '*Mr. S.*'"

"Oh, pshaw,—" Valentine Loft laughed, "those are the two words Mr. Curran spoke that night he was pretending to be clairvoyant. They meant nothing, but they stuck in your subconsciousness, Stella, and wove themselves into your dream."

"I don't remember Mr. Curran's saying them," Stella protested.

"But he did," Loft returned. "And nobody showed any understanding of what he meant. He used them at random. I'm afraid, Stella, your dream can't help us much."

"But I think it does," Miss Dwyer, exclaimed; "of course you men will deny it, but that dream goes to prove, to my mind, that my brother's murder is the result of his possession of books that another collector coveted. I have no doubt Miss Lawrence knows or suspects this, and that is why such a dream came to her. As to the titles of the books, if Mr. Loft's explanation of that is the true one, it makes no difference. Miss Lawrence may have heard my brother use those two words or phrases, and have entirely forgotten it. Then they returned to her in her dream."

"I doubt if Mr. Curran actually made up those words," Kinney said; "I think they meant something to him,—even if no one else present understood them."

"Rosalie, I think,—was the name of his wife," Miss Dwyer said. "At least he sometimes called her that,—or Rose, or Rosy,—yet it is my impression they were all nicknames, and not her real name."

Angel Bob Baldwin had listened to this conversation mostly in silence. Now he took the floor.

"Miss Dwyer," he said, "you have doubtless heard, as you say, of the greed and covetousness of book collectors. And, while it is true to a degree, it is by no means true that they make a practice of killing other collectors in their zeal. I am, in a way, a book dealer,—though I have no shop or store-room. I am more of a commission agent. Yet, I am familiar with the ways of the collectors, especially the most important ones. And I know that no one of them would kill a man or would even resort to dishonest methods to gain a book he desired. There are some, I daresay, who would do so, but not the important, the celebrated collectors. Your brother was one of these, Mr. Loft is one. And I can speak for Mr. Loft when I say that never has he descended to the slightest bit of underhanded dealing to attain a desired volume. Nor did your brother. These two men, as well as all of my clients, are most observant of the rights of fellow collectors. They give me their bids for an auction sale, or a private sale, and I execute their commissions with the same care and honesty that a broker or banker would use in financial transactions. I am telling you this, because I see you are under a misapprehension as to the methods and manners of first-class collectors."

"All very fine, Mr. Baldwin," the lady returned, "except that I don't believe it. I have come here to discover who killed my brother. If it turns out to be one of you men who threatened him—"

"Threatened him!" cried Angel. "What *do* you mean?"

"Well, I'm told you discussed murder,—and what was the best method, and all that."

"We did," Loft said, "but it was no threat,—it was regarding no intended victim! Miss Dwyer, you must be crazy!"

"No, sir, I am not crazy, but I am a determined woman. I shall never rest until I discover the criminal. If the local police cannot accomplish this, I shall engage a private detective—"

"Do so, if you wish, Miss Dwyer." Loft was courteous, as always. "I, too, should be glad to have the mystery solved."

"I'll help you, Miss Dwyer," Stella offered. "I'm not sure that a woman's intuition can't accomplish more than a man's skill. At any rate, I'm glad you do not scoff at my dreams,—for I have too often proved their truth and value to slight their importance."

The two women left the room and Kinney turned to Loft.

"I want to take up that matter of the woman Mr. Meredith told of," he began. "It hasn't been sufficiently considered, I say. Now, Mr. Loft, what women slept on that floor that night?"

"Why on that floor?" objected Loft. "Granting a veiled woman went into Curran's room, late at night, she could have come down from the floor above."

"Or up from the floor below," added Angel. "I hate to seem to asperse the character of a dead man, but Curran was evidently a woman lover of sorts. He was, I can't help thinking,—quite capable of a vulgar intrigue with a housemaid,—and Valhalla employs some very pretty ones."

"It is an unpleasant supposition," Loft said, gravely, "but I'd rather think that, than to imagine any of our own people doing such a thing."

"Who were on that floor?" persisted Kinney.

"Mrs. Meredith, Mrs. Knox, Miss Fuller, Miss Lawrence, the Countess, and Mrs. Jennings, the housekeeper," Loft said shortly. "No one of those is possible. My housekeeper is a staid, middle-aged person, and the other ladies are out of the question. If there was a visitor, such as Mr. Meredith described, it must have been—"

"Tessie, perhaps," Angel suggested.

"Yes, Tessie, if anybody," Loft agreed. "She is a naughty little piece,— Mrs. Jennings has often threatened to discharge her. But she's a capable chambermaid, and such are not easy to get."

"Well, if Tessie did go there that night, she surely didn't kill Curran," Angel said, reflectively. "How could she have done it?"

"Like most theories, it presupposes previous acquaintance with Curran," Kinney said; "whoever killed that man, knew him before. Nobody could have done it on first acquaintance."

"Unless it was Ned Knox," Loft said; "I'm loath to suspect Ned, but you know, Angel, how impulsive he is,—and how jealous of Anna."

Kinney looked disturbed. He hated to have Knox accused,—he hated any reflection on Anna.

"Mr. Knox was the one who advocated shooting," he reminded them.

"That's nothing," Loft said, "he had no pistol up here,—and, too, it was less suspicious to choose the method he had not advocated."

Valentine Loft looked moody and worried. He did not want to accuse Knox, but he had his own reasons for doing so. The man was beset by doubts and fears. He felt the fearful responsibility of this misfortune that had come to him,—and he had a secret cause for anxiety that was driving him to distraction. If Knox should be proved the guilty person, Loft, while not exactly glad, would be greatly relieved.

Miss Dwyer, too, was a nuisance. As Loft was a lawyer, she appealed to him continually in regard to minor legal questions. She declared she would not let him touch her brother's belongings or have anything to do with the settlement of his estate, but she still pestered him with her foolish questions and arguments. Miss Dwyer was by no means sure of the guilt she attributed to Valentine Loft, but she did suspect him, and indomitably she pursued her inquiries.

No will of Hugh Curran had been heard of, so Miss Dwyer was doubtless the sole heir.

Repeatedly Loft advised her to put the whole matter in the hands of a capable attorney,—but the spinster hesitated, her real reason being that if Loft should be freed from her suspicion, he was the lawyer she wished to retain.

So she stayed at Valhalla, bothering every one, annoying every one, but serenely unconscious of it.

The passing days brought no new theories or discoveries on the part of the police. Their knowledge of the circumstances seemed to be complete as far as they could make it. No questioning of household or servant brought any new revelations.

Tessie, when grilled, seemed to be entirely innocent of any acquaintanceship with Hugh Curran. The idea of her tapping on his door that night was the merest surmise. The girl was frank and seemingly truthful.

Moreover, Violet vouched for her presence in the bedroom they shared, soon after half-past one that night.

"She has an alibi," Angel said, as they discussed it after Tessie had been dismissed. "An unshakable alibi,—if Violet tells the truth."

"If," said Kinney.

"I think she does," Loft declared. "They are good girls, and Mrs. Jennings says they are truthful. It's too bad to suspect them with positively no reason for it."

"That's so," Kinney agreed; "we must look elsewhere."

CHAPTER 9

PAULINE'S GRIEF

KINNEY, away from the lure of Anna's presence, wondered how he had been so subjugated by her. The man was soft-hearted but hard-headed, and, thinking it all over, he began to wonder whether she hadn't purposely bamboozled him.

He began to think that it would be quite possible for her story to be all true up to the tap on Curran's door. Or rather to the next statement, which was that Anna was sure the visitor was a woman.

Suppose it had not been a woman at all,—suppose it had been the irate husband, Ned Knox. And suppose Anna, banking on Mr. Meredith's story had added her assurance that the caller was a woman.

The more Kinney pondered over this idea, the more plausible it appeared to him. He decided not to discuss it with anybody, but to ferret it out himself.

For, he had come to the conclusion that the men at Valhalla changed their mental attitudes from day to day. Loft, himself, now suspected Knox and the next day he would disclaim all such possibility.

Kinney concluded finally that he would learn more from the women than from the men.

So he set forth on his day's work by asking an interview with the Countess Galaski.

This self-important personage granted the request, and received him in a small reception room where they could be alone.

"I'm glad you have come to me at last, Mr. Kinney," she said, her black eyes snapping and her over-red lips set in a straight line.

"You know something, madam?" he inquired, surprised.

"I may know something and I may not," she returned, "but at least, I can give you a hint which way to look."

"I hope you will do so, Countess."

"Well,—find Mr. Curran's watch."

"That is one of my chiefest endeavors. If you can give me a hint as to its whereabouts, I shall indeed be grateful."

"I can't do that, Mr. Kinney, but—has it never occurred to you to search the rooms of the household,—guests, servants and all?"

"Why, no,—I confess I've not thought of doing that."

"It might produce results."

"I can't think so, Countess. Supposing for a moment, any one under this roof had taken the watch, such a one would, of course, have disposed of it before this. It's over a week now, since Mr. Curran's death, and no one, I mean no one of criminal intent, would keep any damaging evidence still in possession."

"Nevertheless, it could do no harm to look."

"Then advise me a little further. Look where? There's no use in searching all the rooms, if you have some knowledge,—some inkling of where it may be."

The Countess pondered.

"No;" she said, finally. "I can't advise you. There may be no result whatever, and in that case, I am not willing to mention any name."

"At least, you have given me a new idea, and I thank you, Countess. Do help me further, and tell me when the rooms,—certain rooms are most likely to be vacated. I don't want to advertise this search, as that would lead to greater precautions."

"You'll have to watch for yourself. It should not be difficult. Say, if several go for a motor drive this afternoon, you could go into their rooms then. Or, there is always opportunity while we are at dinner or luncheon."

Kinney looked at her admiringly.

"It may seem to you, Countess, that you are instructing me in matters I should have known myself. But, I admit, a search of the rooms here for the missing watch, never came into my mind,—and, frankly, I don't hope for much from it."

"Maybe not," the Countess smiled, "but it can do no harm. Of course, you will ignore and forget any thing you may learn not bearing on your case."

"Of course," returned Kinney, sincerely. "I may include your room?"

"Oh, yes, if you like; though the fact of my proposing this search would seem to imply my own innocence. However, were I guilty myself, I'd be clever enough to cook up this scheme,—so go ahead. Search my room with the rest."

Kinney was not quite ready to follow this advice without telling Valentine Loft of his intentions, so he went at once in quest of the master of the house.

"Why, of course," Loft said; "go ahead, Kinney. I hate to have it done, but if you think it necessary, proceed."

"I've wondered why you don't do something of the sort," said Baldwin, who was with Loft in the smoking room. "And another thing, Mr. Kinney, why don't you check up alibis?"

"I've tried to, Mr. Baldwin, but at two o'clock in the morning an alibi is a hard thing to prove. Everybody simply says, 'In bed, asleep,' and who's to prove otherwise?"

"That's true," Angel returned. "Mr. Loft and I can vouch for each other, as I'm rooming in his suite, but most of the others are alone."

"That's just it, sir," said Kinney. "Even Mr. Knox was in his own bedroom with the door closed. So his wife can't swear to his alibi."

"Nor he to hers," observed Loft. "Mr. Baldwin and I can swear to each other's presence from one o'clock on, and the Merediths shared a room. Except for us four, every one roomed alone,—that's so."

"That's why I feel I must search the rooms," Kinney stated. "There may be some evidence against somebody, some unexpected clue—"

"Yes, there may be," Angel said; "and here's another thing. I want to look around Curran's room a bit more. His sister has taken away his personal belongings, but I think there might be some clues in the waste basket or on the tables or floor. Roly Mears fancies himself as a detective, but the boy doesn't get anywhere. So, if you've the key, Mr. Kinney, let's run up there a few minutes."

"Very well, sir, I'm willing. Come along."

The two went up the great staircase, and as they turned into the corridor that led to the room Hugh Curran had occupied, they almost fell over pretty Tessie, the maid, who was stooping, her ear at the keyhole of a door.

"Here, you!" cried Kinney roughly, putting out his hand to snatch her away. "What do you mean?"

But to his surprise, instead of looking frightened, Tessie drew herself upright, and finger on lip, motioned Kinney to listen himself at the keyhole.

Surprised into acquiescence the detective did so, and, listening intently, he heard a woman's agonized sobs.

More, he heard broken snatches of sentences, cried out in agony, as if irrepressible wailings of a broken heart.

"If I could only forget!" were the words that came to him, scarcely breathed, almost inaudible, yet he was just able to catch them.

"I will forget!" she went on, after another short period of intense grief. "I must—I will forget!"

And then—in a clear, ringing triumphant voice, "I have forgotten, yes,— I have forgotten!"

Though not loud this was so unmistakably a desperate resolve, a determined achievement, that Kinney could almost see the conquering smile that must have accompanied it.

And yet, the next instant, the speaker broke down again, and sobbed as if her heart would break.

Feeling ashamed of himself, Kinney stood up, and taking Tessie's arm, drew her along with them, and the three entered Hugh Curran's room, as Kinney unlocked the door.

"Now," he said, closing the door, pushing Tessie into a chair, and standing over her with a lowering face.

"Now, what do you mean by eavesdropping like that?"

"It was this way, sir," and Tessie was no whit embarrassed. "That's Miss Fuller's room, and I went up to make it up, sir. At the door, I thought I heard her crying, and I thought I'd better not intrude. I stooped to listen, to make sure she really was crying, and then you came along."

"That's all right," Angel said, nodding at Kinney. "Tessie is a chambermaid on this floor and it was her duty to report for work. If she heard Miss Fuller crying, she did right about hesitating to enter, and though I can't condone listening at keyholes, it seemed the natural thing to do. Is anyone else in the room?"

"I don't know," said Kinney, slowly. "Either there is, or Miss Fuller was talking to herself. She was certainly in deep distress."

"Some one ought to go to her!" exclaimed Bob. "Some of the women."

"I don't think so," Kinney demurred. "She seemed in trouble of her own. She was saying, 'If I could only forget! I must forget!' That sounds like a personal, a private sorrow. I think it better not to intrude. A little later, Tessie may go in,—and perhaps she can be of assistance in some way."

"Miss Fuller has been like that before, sir," Tessie volunteered. "Twice, I've found her crying when I went to help her dress for dinner."

"What was her explanation?" asked Kinney.

"The first time,—she said some dust had flown in her eyes from the window. But I think she knew I didn't believe that. The second time, she said nothing,—just bathed her eyes and let me dress her without a word."

"Then she won't resent your presence now. Run along, Tessie; if you can get in, do all you can for her. If not, come back here and tell us about it."

"Yes, Mr. Kinney," and the astute maid went away.

"That girl knows a lot," said Baldwin. "She's either a good faithful servant, or she's a wily, canny fraud. I don't know which."

"She's both," said Kinney, sapiently. "She's a good servant,—Mr. Loft says so,—but she's mighty cute. Little goes on that she doesn't see."

"Yes, she saw Mrs. Knox on the balcony," Angel reminded him.

"I don't believe she did," and Kinney remembered his promise to Anna. "I think she made that yarn up."

"Good for you," cried Baldwin. "I'm glad to hear you say that. I'd hate to believe any wrong of Mrs. Knox. But get busy, Kinney, and help me look round this place. Hello, where's the book catalogue gone?"

"Which one? Here are two."

"Yes, they're little ones. But there was a big one, it was here that morning,—when we found Mr. Curran."

"Do you want it? I suppose it can be found. Probably Mr. Loft took it,—or maybe Miss Dwyer. She wants to sell the books of her brother, you know."

"It doesn't matter. I can get another like it. Now let's hunt the waste basket. There are always clues in a waste basket. Or, I'll look in it, while you search the bureau drawers. I can't help feeling there are clues to be found in his room."

Bob bent over the basket and Kinney obediently searched the drawers of dresser and chiffonier.

"Nothing doing," the detective said, at last, turning to the other. "You found anything?"

He smiled at the heap of litter Bob had turned out on the floor.

"No," was the perplexed reply.

"Looking for anything in particular? You seem disappointed."

"I am disappointed, but I'm not after anything in particular. Except I hoped to find some letter or note that might tell us something. Come on, I've searched all I want to. I don't think so much of waste basket clues after all. I can find no 'feathers left around' at all."

They went away, and a slight pause at the door of Pauline Fuller's room brought no sound to the ears of the detective.

"All quiet in here now," he said, rather soberly, as they went downstairs.

And at the luncheon table, Bob, to his surprise, found Pauline in an unusually gay mood. She was talkative and animated, and her good spirits infected the others, until the atmosphere became more cheery and bright than it had been since the occurrence of the tragedy.

Luncheon over, Bob took possession of Little Anna and carried her off for a stroll in the gardens.

"I just want to tell you, dear," Angel said, "that I, for one, do not believe that yarn of Tessie's about you."

"You blessed Angel!" and Anna gave him her loveliest smile. "I'm glad I have at least one friend at court."

"And so," Bob went on, "that lets Ned out as a suspect. For though you did make a few eyes at Curran during the evening, that wasn't enough to rouse jealous old Ned to the killing pitch."

"Of course it wasn't," and Anna beamed satisfaction. "Now, Angel, who did do it?"

"Anna,—look here. Ned is out of it,—I'm vouched for by Valentine himself, so I'm out of it. Now, there's only one left of the trio who discussed ways and means—"

"Val himself!" said Anna, softly. "But why, Angel, for Heaven's sake, *why?*"

"I don't know,—but,—oh, Anna, I can't say it,—but do you think, can you imagine that Pauline knew Curran before?"

Anna looked both serious and frightened.

"I wouldn't think so, Angel, only,—when Mr. Curran did that mind reading stunt,—Pauline did look self-conscious."

"At what?"

"I think it was at 'Mr. S.' You know, Hugh Curran flung out 'Mr. S.', and 'Rosalie,' and—now, Angel, don't kill me! but I felt sure that Pauline turned white and gripped at her chair arms when he said, 'Mr. S.' and—yes, I will tell you,—I thought you did, Bob, when he said 'Rosalie'! Did you?"

"Did I? I did not! I never knew anybody named Rosalie in my life. I never heard the name except in some general way. But, Anna, that 'Rosalie' has been explained. It seems it was his wife's name, or nickname. His sister said so."

"Yes,—I know. But he didn't say it that night because it was his wife's name. Nobody here ever heard of his wife. He used it to tease somebody and I thought it might be you."

"Well it wasn't. Maybe Val knows some Rosalie person,—or maybe your Ned does,—I don't."

"Ned doesn't either, I asked him. Well, it's no matter anyway. But I'm positive Pauline was upset at the mention of 'Mr. S.' and that's why I thought maybe she had known Mr. Curran before. Or maybe she knew some 'Mr. S.' who also knew Mr. Curran."

"Maybe," said Bob. "Anyway, Pauline was in high spirits at lunch time."

"Put on," and Anna wagged her head sagaciously. "I know Pauline,—and the worse she feels, the gayer she acts,—I mean, if she doesn't want people to know."

Baldwin thought of Kinney's account of Pauline's grief that morning, and he wondered.

"You're sure, Anna?" he inquired.

"Positive. And, too, I know Pauline had been crying. She had on an extra touch of rouge, but she couldn't entirely correct her reddened eyelids. Whatever was the matter, she cried over it. Then she made a very careful toilette, dressed her hair and fixed up her face with greatest care,—but she couldn't fool me. She had had one good big cry this morning, that I know."

"Oh, well, I suppose you women all have your ups and downs."

"Of course, and it's enough to make Pauly cry to have all this horror here, so shortly before her wedding day."

"Is the day set?"

"Not quite, but it will be inside a couple of months. That is, it would have been. I don't know whether this horrid business will postpone it or not. But, Angel, nobody seems to get anywhere. Why is nothing being done?"

"It's a hard nut to crack, Anna. And the wheels of justice move slowly—"

"They don't move at all! I'm trying to get Ned to take me away."

"He can't, Anna, until he is freed from suspicion."

"Ned! Suspicion! Ridiculous!"

"Ridiculous, I grant, but that Dwyer woman holds that all of us, Ned, Val, and myself are under suspicion, because of that fool talk we had—"

"But you've just said Val can prove your alibi."

"I know,—but I can't prove his. You see, the house was crowded that night, and I went into Val's suite. I slept in his bed,—he would have it so,—and he slept on the couch in his sitting room. So,—the way the rooms are,—he could go out into the hall if he wished, and I wouldn't know it,—unless I heard him—"

"The door was closed between you two?"

"Yes; and the room he slept in opens out to the hall, but the bedroom where I was, doesn't. So that, if he stepped carefully, he could easily go out and return without my knowing it; whereas, I couldn't get out to the hall, without going through the room where he slept. And he's a very light sleeper,—so there's my alibi. Besides, I didn't go out, or try to go out at all."

"Of course you didn't. Why would you kill Curran?"

"It isn't the why, Anna, it's the who? Why would Val kill him? And yet, if it really was one of us three, and if you take Ned out, and if Val proved my alibi, there's no one left but Val."

"Rubbish, it never was Val!"

"No, I don't think it was either."

Yet it was not long before Angel Bob had an opportunity to revise his opinion.

On their return to the house, Roly Mears beckoned to Bob, excitedly.

"Come on, old chap," he said, in a low tone; "come on, quick."

Leaving Anna with the others, Bob followed Roly, who took him to the library, where Kinney was waiting.

"Mr. Kinney has found something, Angel," Roly said. "I don't want to tell Val, or anybody, until you hear about it. Tell him, Mr. Kinney."

"While you were all at luncheon," Kinney began, his face expressing an unwillingness to divulge the secret he had, "I made some search among the bedrooms. I hated to do it, but it had to be done. I looked in the ladies' rooms first, so as to be sure to get that done while they were absent, and in the rooms of the Countess, Miss Lawrence and Miss Dwyer, I found nothing of any informative importance. But,—when I went into Miss Fuller's room,—I did."

"What did you find?" asked Baldwin. He tried to make his voice casual but it shook a little in spite of himself. Was the beautiful Pauline to be dragged into this miserable business?

"I can't think it was anything incriminating," he added.

"It seems to me it is, sir," and Kinney looked as sorrowful as Angel himself.

As he spoke, he handed over to Bob a watch.

It was gold, very thin, and it had no chain or fob attached.

He took it mechanically. Before he examined it at all, he knew it must be Hugh Curran's watch, and the conviction jarred him terribly.

"It is Mr. Curran's?" he asked, staring at the timepiece.

"Yes, Mr. Baldwin. Hidden in a small desk which was locked."

"And which you pried open?"

"And which I opened with a skeleton key. I had to. It was necessary in the interest of justice."

"Damn you and your justice! How dare you break into a lady's locked desk?"

"Softly, now, Mr. Baldwin. That is the duty of a detective. And the fact of its being there, locked up, proves it a secret of Miss Fuller's."

"Secret nothing! If this watch was in Miss Fuller's room, it had a right there. Mr. Curran must have given it to her."

"Very good, sir. That may be. And, now, Mr. Baldwin, if you'll just look at the picture in the watch case—"

Unwilling, yet urged on by the impatient glances of both Kinney and Roly Mears, Angel Bob clicked open the back of Hugh Curran's watch.

And found himself looking on the beautiful face of Pauline Fuller.

Stunned, aghast, he quickly snapped it shut, and stared at Mears.

"What does it mean?" he whispered. His bravado was gone, his face took on a frightened pallor. Angel was emotional, his quick mind saw into the past, turned, saw into the future, and both looked so black, he groaned aloud.

"Val!" he cried, in anguish, "Valentine! Oh, Pauline!"

CHAPTER 10

CURRAN'S WATCH

IT was a moment before Baldwin could pull himself together.

"I can't seem to sense it," he said, musingly. "That watch,—hidden in Miss Fuller's room! Oh,—I see,—it's a plant!"

"A plant?" inquired Roly.

"Yes,—somebody has done it to drag Pauline into this mess,—or, the criminal is trying to divert suspicion from himself—"

"Herself!" Mears exclaimed; "if your suggestion is true, that's a woman's trick! And, it may be mere mischief—do you suppose Anna—"

"Oh, hush, Roly," Bob exclaimed. "Why harp on Anna?"

"But there's more to this than meets the eye. You see, Angel, if Ned killed Curran because he flirted with Anna, then Anna is going to use every means to turn suspicion from Ned."

"It looks like that to me," Detective Kinney agreed. "To my way of thinking, Mr. Knox is the only one who seems to have a motive—"

"*Seems* to have,—perhaps," Roly said; "but anybody else may have a motive of which we know nothing. Ned Knox is impulsive, impetuous,—but I can't believe he'd murder,—just because of a flirtation—"

"We don't know, Mr. Mears," Kinney reminded him, "just how serious that flirtation was. Men *have* killed other men, when they found them—"

"Never mind,—don't speculate," Roly said; "now, Angel, what is the thing to do,—regarding the watch, I mean?"

"Take it straight to Val," Baldwin replied, promptly. "It's the only thing to do. We can't speak of it to Pauline,—I don't for a minute believe she knows a thing about it—"

"Now, now, Mr. Baldwin, I think she does," Kinney spoke gravely. "It's all very well to hold a lady above suspicion,—but I can't see how the murderer could get that watch into Miss Fuller's locked desk—"

"Don't speculate, let's find out. I say, show the watch to Mr. Loft, tell him the whole story, and do as he says. Give him the first chance to clear Miss Fuller—for, she must be cleared."

"I'd rather put it up to the lady herself," the detective demurred.

"Well, you can't." Angel Bob was dominating. "If she knows nothing of it, we must find out who does,—and if Miss Fuller is in any way implicated, it will come out soon enough. Mr. Loft is the right one to go to, for he will want to shield Miss Fuller from any unpleasantness possible."

Kinney looked a little surprised at the methods that seemed to obtain among gentlemen, but he was willing to take the matter to Valentine Loft, and said so.

"Come on, then," and with the amazed look still on his face, Baldwin led the way.

They found Loft and beckoned to him, and the four men went into the library and shut the door.

"What is it?" Loft asked; "anything new?"

His lean, strong face looked careworn, his expression was not hopeful. As a matter of fact, he was pretty well bowled over by the misfortune that had fallen on his house. He dreaded any solution of the mystery,—for he could conceive of none that would not implicate some of his friends or guests, and he wanted, most of all, to be rid of the whole business.

But a glance at the faces of those about him now, showed him that there was something of importance to be divulged.

"Out with it," he said; "you have found something, I see."

"Yes," said Kinney, "we have found Hugh Curran's watch."

"Whose picture is in it?" Loft asked, quickly. "Anna's?"

He bit his lip, annoyed at his own impulsive question. He wouldn't have minded Bob and Roly, but he was truly sorry to have made the suggestion before Kinney.

However, the detective showed no interest in Anna's name, but he watched Loft closely as he handed the watch to him.

Snapping open the back case, Valentine Loft saw the picture of Pauline.

It was not a recent one,—clearly it had been taken a few years since, but it was unmistakable.

The beautiful smiling face was happy and even roguish. A different Pauline from the dignified, gracious woman they knew,—a girl Pauline, almost childish in her innocent smile.

Loft gazed as if hypnotized.

Had it been less tragic it would have been almost comical to note the mild wonder in his face as he turned it to his two friends, ignoring the detective entirely.

"Where do you suppose Curran ever got Pauly's picture?" he said; "such a good one, too,—when she was a little girl,—almost."

"It doesn't mean anything to you, then, Mr. Loft?" Kinney asked, staring hard at him.

"Mean anything? It means that somehow Mr. Curran became possessed of Miss Fuller's picture,—and as it was so beautiful, he kept it."

"She didn't give it to him?"

"She never saw him until she met him here. She told me so herself."

The calm finality of Loft's tone left no room for doubt of his utter belief in his fiancée's word.

"Well, Mr. Loft, I'm sorry to tell you that I found the watch, hidden in a locked desk in Miss Fuller's room."

"Who put it there?" Loft's tone was quiet, but the men who knew him could see a gleam come into his eye.

"We don't know," Kinney spoke almost gently, "but in my opinion, Miss Fuller put it there herself."

"Mr. Kinney," Loft spoke very sternly, "if you mean she did so with some unexplained but innocent intent, very well. If, however, you are implying or suggesting a shade of doubt or suspicion of Miss Fuller—in any way,—you will answer to me for it! How dare you," he went on, as Kinney's face told plainly that he had his suspicions, "how dare you even speak the name of that lady in connection with wrong-doing of any sort? I—I could kill you where you sit!"

"Now, Val," Angel interrupted, "don't sling around any more remarks about killing! We're too careless in the way we use that word. You're not going to kill Mr. Kinney,—and you must listen, if he has any theories to offer. Good Heavens, man, his words,—whatever they might be,—couldn't hurt Pauline!"

"No; but they hurt me! They infuriate me! I won't have it! Retract, Mr. Kinney, or leave my house this instant!"

"I haven't said anything yet," Kinney reminded him; "and, too, Mr. Loft, as an agent of the Law, I can't be ordered out of a house, even by its owner."

"Law or no law, I'll put you out myself, if you mention the lady's name again,—in any connection whatever!"

"Why, Val," cried Mears, "I've never seen you excited before! Don't take it like that!"

"There's only one way to take it,—to quash it!" Loft stormed on; "I repeat, if you found that watch in Miss Fuller's room,—it was put there by some evil-minded individual, either to make trouble for Miss Fuller, or to save his own skin! The murderer of Hugh Curran put it there, I have no doubt,—and as to why or how he did it,—I don't know and don't care! I will say, however, Mr. Kinney, that you have done nothing since your arrival,— that you have discovered nothing. That you are making trouble instead of curing it, and that unless you agree to drop this particular phase of the matter I shall take steps to have you removed—in the name of the Law!"

"Fine talk, sir," said Kinney, who grew calmer as Loft grew more excited. "Fine talk, but it gets you nowhere. Why not face facts, Mr. Loft? Why not accept the fact that I found the watch,—as I said,—and let me confront

Miss Fuller with the fact, and receive her doubtless satisfactory explanation of its presence in her locked desk."

Valentine Loft looked at the speaker with a glance of utter disdain.

"You shall never have an interview of any sort with Miss Fuller," he said, more quietly than he had yet spoken. "If the watch must be shown to her, or discussed with her,—I will do it,—no one else may."

"I'm afraid I'll have to insist on being present at that interview, Mr. Loft," and the detective shook his head doggedly.

"You shall not! You sneaking, spying—"

"Now, Valentine," Angel Bob seemed almost alarmed, "let up on all that. I know how you feel about Pauline, but can't you see, man, that all your bluster and anger doesn't help her cause any? In fact, it strengthens any possible suspicion against—"

"Don't dare say it, Bob!" Loft's eyes were blazing, and he turned on Baldwin in fierce anger. "I am blustering,—I know it. I never blustered before in my life,—I never had occasion to! But this!"

Loft stopped suddenly, and again looked at the picture in the watch which he still held in his hand.

As he gazed, his face softened, his features relaxed into a half smile, and he said, at last:

"This must have been taken when Pauly was a school girl. She can't be more than eighteen, here. I daresay she gave it to some school chum, and Curran got possession of it merely as a fancy picture. For he never knew Pauly. I'll go to her,—she'll tell me all about it,—but you must let me go alone, Mr. Kinney. I'll agree, on my honor, to tell you all she says, but I really don't want an audience to our conversation."

Loft had calmed down to his usual composure, and his voice was tranquil again. Having hit on what seemed to him an adequate solution of the picture in Curran's watch, he was ready to treat Kinney in his former friendly manner.

The two men were not at all congenial,—the detective's blunt business manners were distasteful to Loft's suave culture, but if Pauline's name could be stricken from the detective's slate, Loft would let him run his own gait in peace.

"Will you go and inquire about the matter at once, Mr. Loft?" Kinney asked.

"I will do it during the afternoon, Mr. Kinney. Not just at the moment, for I chance to know that Miss Fuller has gone to her room for a nap. I am not willing to disturb her,—it is her habit to rest after luncheon. But I will arrange to see her this afternoon sometime, and I will take up the subject with her. Meantime, I will keep the watch."

"No, Mr. Loft, I will keep the watch. It is a piece of material evidence,— at least, as things stand now."

"A feather left around," said Roly, smiling. "Let him keep it, Val,—he has the right to."

"It doesn't matter," and Loft handed the watch back to the detective, with a faint shrug of his shoulders, as if, after all, the incident was of small account.

"You'd do well to adopt a maxim of mine, Kinney," he said. "It is, 'Do nothing and all will be done.' Ever hear it before?"

"No, and I never want to again. I'd get nowhere at all, if I worked on that line, Mr. Loft."

"That's where you make your mistake. There are many times when a masterly inactivity brings about the best results. This is one of them. Do nothing in that watch matter,—it will all be done. I'll meet you here, say, at five o'clock,—it's three, now,—and I'll prove my statement."

And with this Kinney was forced to be content.

Unable to find better company he attached himself to Miss Dwyer.

She was always ready to talk to him, but he rarely gained any information from her.

This time, however, she had something on her mind.

"I have a theory, Mr. Kinney," she said, her pale blue eyes blinking with earnestness, "and it's this. You see, my brother was killed by somebody in this house. None of the servants did it,—that's too ridiculous! So, it was some of the household themselves,—or guests, I mean. Well, not one of them knew my brother, or had any personal motive to kill him. But, he was a great and successful book collector. So, I am sure the motive was possession of his rare volumes. To you this may seem an inadequate motive,—but I assure you it is not. I know, Mr. Baldwin says that the big collectors don't kill to get the treasures,—but he may be mistaken in this instance, and, too, Mr. Loft isn't a very big collector."

"Oh, so it's Mr. Loft you are favoring with your suspicions, is it? But, Mr. Baldwin is also interested in books."

"Not in the same way. You don't know about such matters, I daresay,— but the collector's mania is really a dangerous thing. Mr. Baldwin wants books to buy and then to sell to another customer. He doesn't have that craving to possess that besets the collector. It is a desperate covetousness, an insane envy that leads to any lengths to get the desired book. I know, for I know how it affected my brother. He never committed crime, but I know,—ah, I know that he resorted to means not—not strictly honorable."

"All very interesting, Miss Dwyer, but we have no evidence. You see both Mr. Loft and Mr. Baldwin were in their rooms all night, after one o'clock or so."

"You've only their word for that."

Kinney looked at her, startled. It was true,—if Loft and Baldwin had been disposed, they could have acted in collusion, and could have accomplished the deed more easily than any one else. If there were any way to get in and out of that locked door, Loft would know about his own house.

Kinney had sneaking suspicions of a secret passage somewhere, but his closest scrutiny had been unable to find any trace of such.

He put Miss Hetty's suggestion away in his brain to think about later, and said:

"What does Mr. Curran's fiancée look like?"

"Just a pretty young thing."

"Does she look at all like Miss Fuller?"

"Not the least mite,—almost her opposite. Why?"

"Nothing. Why didn't he carry her picture in his watch?"

"I don't know. Maybe he did. I'm told his watch was stolen from him, wasn't it?"

"It was missing when the body was found," Kinney evaded, "but he might have put it away himself."

As the pair talked, a few others had come out on the terrace, and the Countess, passing, heard the word "watch."

"Found it?" she said, quickly, seating herself by Kinney. "I told you to look for that watch."

"Why,"—and Kinney looked at her curiously.

"Because it might easily prove indicative. And I know you've found it, Mr. Kinney! Your countenance is not always under control, and I'm sure you've found it! Where was it?"

Kinney was taken aback, but he was quick-witted at times, and he replied, easily:

"No such luck, Countess Galaski. It may turn up,—but I searched several places without success."

Miss Hetty Dwyer, never at ease in the presence of the caustic Countess had walked away, and glancing around to be sure no one else was listening, the Countess went on:

"You would do well, Mr. Kinney, to take me into your confidence. I could be of real help to you."

Kinney was a little weary of offers of help from women, but he never dared neglect a possible bit of assistance.

"I've nothing particular to confide, ma'am, but if you've any helpful information it's your duty to give it out."

"Not information,—merely advice. And here it is,—if you want it bluntly. Beware of that little Mrs. Knox. I know how she is pulling wool over your eyes—"

"What?"

Kinney was so surprised that he quite forgot his manners.

"Yes,—that's just what she does to everybody."

"Ah," Kinney thought to himself, "feminine jealousy."

"I don't care how much she flirts or with whom," the lady went on, "but I want you to be on your guard when she comes to giving you information about—about that night."

"Oh, I know all she can tell me," Kinney shrugged his shoulders. "Know all about that balcony episode, and while it may be a straw to show which way the wind blows,—I don't think it is. Nor can I see her husband in such a rage that he would poison the man who was flirting with her. In a frenzy of jealous passion a man might shoot or stab,—but he couldn't poison."

"Rubbish!" the Countess snapped. "I don't say that he did,—but it's foolish to say that he couldn't. Whoever gave that poison to Mr. Curran did it in some diabolically clever manner. Yet it was done. Now, one could do it as well as another."

"How about some one interested in books?" Kinney asked, remembering Miss Dwyer's talk.

"I think it's as plausible a motive as jealousy," the Countess replied. "But why bother with motive,—find your criminal and then you'll know the motive."

Kinney smiled. "I'd be glad to find either criminal or motive. It's the most ungetatable case I ever handled. I can suspect everybody yet I can suspect nobody. Every one is apparently frank and outspoken, yet also everybody is unwilling to talk about the case."

"Of course nobody wants to talk about the awful affair if it can be helped. But I'm sure we all want to tell you anything you may wish to ask."

"Very well, then, Countess Galaski, do you suspect any one,—any one at all?"

After a pause, the Countess said, slowly: "Yes, I think I do."

"Will you tell me who it is?"

"It is 'Rosalie'."

"But—'Rosalie,' that is the name of Mr. Curran's divorced wife. She isn't here."

"I don't mean Rosalie in person,—I mean the one who was in Mr. Curran's mind, when he spoke the name of Rosalie that night."

"But,—I've heard it rumored that Mr. Baldwin was disturbed when Mr. Curran mentioned that name."

"The rumors are wrong then. It was not Mr. Baldwin who was self-conscious at the name of Rosalie."

"No? Who was, then?"

"That I shall not tell. I may be all wrong,—I wouldn't for the world attract attention to the wrong person. But, take my word for it, Mr. Curran had no thought of Bob Baldwin, when he said, 'Rosalie.' I thought Mr. Baldwin looked a little annoyed at the name of 'Mr. S.' But I'm not sure. I may be mistaken as to that. But to return to my well-meant warning, don't believe all Mrs. Knox tells you. She is a spiteful little cat, and while she is not exactly in love with Valentine Loft, she takes delight in trying to stir up trouble between him and Miss Fuller."

"She hasn't succeeded as yet," said Kinney, remembering Loft's valiant defence of his fiancée.

"No,—but she will if she can. She's a little devil,—loves mischief for the sheer fun of it!"

"Pleasant character!"

"Oh, she's so pretty and charming and innocent of appearance she is beloved of all."

Kinney went off by himself and found he had plenty to meditate upon until five o'clock, when he was due to meet Loft in the library.

He went there, and found the master of Valhalla waiting for him. No one else was present, and Loft carefully shut the door.

"Mr. Kinney," he began, "I am in very grave trouble. As I promised you, I tried to obtain an interview with Miss Fuller. But Miss Fuller has gone away."

"Run away!" Kinney almost shouted.

"Gone away," I said. "Pray, be quiet. I am myself at my wits' end, but I realize it is necessary to consider very carefully our next step."

"Our next step is to find Miss Fuller."

"I'm glad you agree with me. It certainly is. Now, Mr. Kinney, will you undertake to find her? Or would you prefer that I should get another—a private detective to do that? Also, I want no publicity. I want it given out that Miss Fuller has gone home for a rest,—or, gone away on a visit. I do not want it known that her departure was made hastily and secretly."

"I can't keep it so dark, Mr. Loft. We can't find her without publicity. Look at the thing yourself. We find the watch in her possession, locked in her desk. We take the watch,—she discovers it is gone and she seeks safety in flight. What's the answer?"

Valentine Loft showed none of the indignation and anger he had displayed in the morning.

"I don't know the answer," he returned, quietly; "but I do know Miss Fuller. She may be the victim of distressing circumstances, but there is no stigma of wrong possible in connection with her name. Now, she must be found. How shall we set about it?"

CHAPTER 11

PAULINE'S FLIGHT

LOFT had sent for Angel, feeling that he wanted a friend to confer with.

"Pauly's gone away," he said briefly, as Baldwin entered the library.

Angel gave him a quick glance, but said, merely,

"Where to?"

"I don't know," Loft returned. "In fact, Angel, she went without my knowing it. I tried to find her just now, but she has gone off in the little car."

"Who took her?"

"Bates, and Tessie went with her. The housekeeper told me all this but she knew nothing more. Bates ought to be back by this time, if Pauline went to the Railway Station, and the housekeeper thinks she did."

"Well, we can't wait for any Bates," Kinney broke in, impatiently. "I know, Mr. Loft, how you hate publicity and all that, but Miss Fuller has been doing queer things——"

"What do you mean by queer things?" Loft spoke quietly, but there was a steely gleam in his eye that Angel knew meant battle. "Miss Fuller has done nothing that you know of. You have no proof that she took Mr. Curran's watch, or that she ever saw the thing. There is a deep-minded criminal behind all this business, and it is not a woman. Some daring and ingenious villain entered my house, killed Hugh Curran and tried to fasten the blame on Miss Fuller. That's the way I see it."

"And that's the way I should see it, if I were the young lady's intended, as you are," Kinney returned, dryly. "But being a detective,—not a great one, but at least, a clear-headed one, I say that when a 'feather left around' is hidden in her own bedroom, and when it is taken from its hiding place, she misses it and immediately disappears herself;—then my clear-sightedness leads me to think she ought to be looked up."

"No one wants to 'look her up' more than I do," Loft said, earnestly. "And, as a bit of disinterested advice, Kinney,—"

"Excuse me, Mr. Loft, you're not capable of giving disinterested advice just now. And, excuse me again, I don't want it. My duty is to find Miss Fuller. My intention is to do it in my own way."

"But, I say, Kinney," Angel put in, "if Mr. Loft wants to find the lady, I'm sure his method of search will be more successful than any you can attempt."

"Sure you may be, sir, but that makes no difference to me. I know my duty, and I'm going to do it. Now, it's true, the hunt for Miss Fuller may mean publicity, may mean police procedure, but I'll promise you this, I'll keep it as quiet as I can. If you want to help,—where do you think she'd go, Mr. Loft?"

"Here's the car," Angel cried, looking from the window. "Bates can surely tell us something."

Bates and Tessie were called in, and Loft asked the chauffeur what Miss Fuller had said.

"She sent Tessie to me," Bates replied, "and said she'd like the little car to go to the station for the four-forty-five. So I was at the door, and she and Tessie got in the car, and we went to the station. There she bid me get her a ticket to New York and a chair. I did that, and then when the train came in she got on it. That's all I know, Mr. Loft."

"Well, Tessie," the detective spoke this time, "what can you tell us about Miss Fuller's journey?"

"Nothing, sir," and though not impertinent, Tessie looked mutinous.

"Detail all she said to you, as she prepared to go," Kinney ordered, sternly.

"Why, she only said, 'I'm going to New York, Tessie. Pack me an overnight bag.' And I did."

"What did you put in it?"

"Only her night things and toilet articles."

"No dresses? No jewels?"

"No, sir, just enough for a night's stay,—without dressing for dinner."

"H'm,—looks bad. Now, didn't Miss Fuller say a word,—while you were helping her dress,—about her plans?"

"Not a word, sir."

"Do you mean she said nothing at all,—or nothing about her plans?"

Tessie considered. "I don't remember her saying anything at all. If she did it was only to direct me what gown she wanted to wear,—or what shoes."

"What did she wear?"

"A black Canton crêpe, with cape to match,—and a black hat with a small veil."

"Inconspicuous costume,—naturally. She took a lot of money with her?"

"I don't know. She always carries a small handbag which she packs herself."

"All her money and jewels in that, of course. Well, Mr. Loft, I doubt if you'll see Miss Fuller again very soon."

"Is that your opinion, Mr. Kinney? Be good enough not to express it to me again. Tessie, you may go. Wait a moment, tell me,—did Miss Fuller say nothing at all that gave you any indication of why she went, or how long she meant to stay?"

"No, sir, not a word." Tessie's eyes filled with tears and she resorted to her handkerchief.

"And," Loft's voice shook a little, "did she give you any—any message for me? You may speak right out before these gentlemen."

"Yes, she did!" and now Tessie sobbed openly, "she said to tell you 'Good-by,' that's all, sir, just 'Good-by.'"

"Very well, Tessie, you may go."

Valentine Loft had perfect control now of his voice, and he nodded a dismissal to Bates, who stood at attention.

But Angel could read the despair in his eyes, the distress in his tense-drawn lips, and he knew that his friend's soul was tasting the torments of hell.

Yet Loft turned a calm face to Kinney, and said, "What is your plan? What would be your idea of efficient search?"

"I'll tell you, sir. We know the lady took the four-forty-five to New York. We've only to wire the police authorities along the route to hold her if she leaves the train before she reaches the city. She won't, though. In all probability, she'll make straight for the metropolis, knowing she can lose herself there easier than in a small town. She's a deep one,—that one!"

"Omit your comments on the lady, if you please, Mr. Kinney." Loft's tone was icy but his eyes blazed fire.

Angel looked at him with some apprehension, for he feared a real explosion if Kinney irritated him much further.

"All right, sir. Nothing personal meant. Well, say we head her off in New York, and then just have her followed,—that's better than an immediate arrest."

"Yes, much better," said Loft, in such a dry way, that Angel turned quickly to look at him. And the slight smile on Loft's face puzzled him.

"You see, Mr. Loft," Kinney went on, "I'm interested in Miss Fuller for more reasons than one. I may as well tell you that I heard her sobbing and weeping in her room,—and crying out, 'I must forget! How *can* I forget?' and after a time, as if by sheer will power, 'I have forgotten!' Now, I can construct a pretty little theory, that in a girlish flirtation, Miss Fuller once gave her picture to Mr. Curran, and——"

"Go, Mr. Kinney," Loft rose and pointed to the door; "go, and take your pretty little theories with you! I may see you later,—though I'd rather not, unless absolutely necessary,—but in any case, I can't stand any more just now. Go."

The upraised voice, the steady, pointing finger, rather awed Kinney, for there was no touch of melodrama about Loft. He merely had reached the end of his rope, and said so.

As the door closed behind the detective, Angel asked:

"Why did you smile, Val?"

"At that fool detective. You know, Pauly never went to New York. If she took a ticket for New York it's a dead certainty that she left the train after a few stops, and went the other way,—to Boston or Albany. I know Pauline so well, that I can read her mental workings. If she wants to disappear,—and it must be, Angel, that she does,—then she would do it more cleverly than any one in the world."

"You're right,—of course. But what does it all mean, Val?"

"I don't know,—but it is serious, very serious. I shan't let Kinney know I think it so, but it is. Any advice, Angel?"

"Not yet,—maybe I can dope some out. But all my sympathy, old chap, and all my help,—at least, all my efforts. What can I do?"

"I don't know. I never in my life felt so helpless. What's all that about Pauly's crying in her room,—and wanting to 'forget'?"

"Do you suppose,—you know, Val, if I'm to help we must be entirely frank,—do you suppose she did know Curran before?"

"I know she didn't,—for she told me so." Loft spoke simply. "I shall always believe her word against all the witnesses or evidence in the whole world. If she had known Curran before, she would have told me so."

"Of course," said Angel, but his acquiescence was based upon his desire to agree with his friend rather than on his faith in feminine candor.

"What about that Rosalie and Mr. S. business," Loft went on, wrinkling his eyebrows. "I've never spoken of it before, but it seemed to me Pauly winced at one of those names."

"Which one—?"

"I don't remember. Mr. S., I suppose,—there's nothing to alarm a woman in another woman's name."

"Was she alarmed?"

"Not quite, but I'm so sensitive to any change of expression on her face, that I thought I observed a little tremor of surprise or annoyance. It probably meant nothing,—"

"But it would presuppose a knowledge of Curran in some way," Angel added, meditatively. "Suppose she did know him before, Val; suppose she didn't tell you of it,—would it make any difference in your feeling toward her?"

"In my feeling toward Pauline! I should say *not*! Why, if she told me all the lies in the catalogue,—or wherever lies grow,—it would make no difference in my feelings toward her! She couldn't do it,—Pauline is incapable of a real lie,—but if she did,—I'd love her exactly the same,—more, if it were possible,—which it isn't. You see, Angel, you don't know from experience what love is. The kind of love I mean. The love that is only possible between—"

"Yes, I know,—two souls that beat as one."

"No, two souls that know how to beat as one. My boy, all hearts can love,—but only hearts that have accompanying brains can get the most and best out of love."

"Well, as long as you have faith in her—"

"Which will be as long as I breathe. Nothing could ever rock my faith in Pauly. She knows this,—and that is why her disappearance alarms me. That is why I know it is very serious. She knows I would forgive her anything—"

"Even murder?"

"It's hard to forgive you that speech, Angel,—but, yes, even murder. It would be a poor love that wouldn't forgive crime. That would be easier to forgive than some other things."

"Such as?"

"Deception,—untruthfulness—"

"Lying—"

"Yes,—real lying,—with intent to deceive me. But I would forgive Pauline that,—anything,—*anything*—"

"Then she will come back."

"No,—she will not come back. She told Tessie to tell me good-bye. But I shall find her."

"She might have told Tessie to say that; if she was merely off on a short errand."

"No; she has told me twice,—that if ever she disappeared suddenly, and sent me the mere message, 'Good-by,' that I never should see her again. I only laughed at the speech,—but I see now that she meant it."

"Then she had a secret, Val."

"It may be." Loft looked straight into Angel's eyes. "Now to find her," he said, after a moment's pause.

"Where do you think she can be?"

"I know where she is."

"And you can find her?"

"No; but I know this. She started on the New York train. She got off at some way station. She crossed the tracks and took a train on the other side, in the other direction, and after travelling some time she will get out at some inconspicuous town or village,—where she knows some friend who will hide her successfully for as long as she wishes to be hidden."

"Good Heavens, then how can you find her?"

"The hardest situation to solve,—I know that. But she can never be traced through her bankers or her home people or her lawyers. I am sure of that."

"I didn't know Pauline was so extraordinarily clever."

"It isn't so much cleverness as common sense. A more ingenious brain might plan to hide in a big city,—it is conceded the best place. But it isn't.

Granting a discreet and loving friend, in a secluded country home, Pauly's plan is the best. And she has plenty of such friends. But I shall find her."

"Maybe she doesn't want to be found."

"But I want to find her. I want Pauline."

"Where is her aunt, now?"

"In the New York house. But she is ill and nervous, and in the care of nurses. She'll see no papers,—even if they carry the story,—and unless I hear from the house, I shall send no message."

"Has Pauline no other relatives?"

"Only some distant cousins. She is her own mistress, and she comes and goes as she pleases. If Kinney would keep his mouth shut, her absence from here would never be known."

But Kinney didn't keep his mouth shut. On the contrary, he opened it very often, indeed. Already he had quizzed the guests and the servants over the entire house. Already he had telephoned orders to follow Pauline if she could be discovered anywhere *en route* to New York.

Already he had made up his mind that Pauline Fuller had killed Hugh Curran,—but this decision he had the grace to keep to himself and used his busy mouth merely for asking questions.

Miss Hetty Dwyer was greatly excited.

"Now, perhaps you will do something," she cried. "I've had my suspicions of that sly Pauline all the way along. Her, with her long, dark eyes and her thin red lips! I've my opinion of her! And her picture in my brother's watch all the time! The hussy! I'll bet she knew him since he was engaged to Miss Fitzgerald! Made trouble between 'em, like as not! You'll catch her, won't you, Mr. Kinney?"

"I hope so," he returned. "But I thought you suspected a criminal Book Collector, Miss Dwyer?"

"Oh, Lord, I don't suspect Miss Fuller of killing Hugh! No,—she's a sly devil, but not bad enough for that. I can't conceive of a woman murderer! But she has some reason for running away that's connected with the crime, I'll bet on that!"

"Don't you remember," Anna said, reminiscently, "almost as soon as Mr. Curran got here, he asked Pauline to walk in the garden with him—alone?"

"What a strange thing to do!" cried Miss Hetty.

"Not at all," the Countess defended. "He was a guest, and Pauline was a charming hostess,—it wasn't a bit strange."

"Well, I'll tell you what was strange," said Stella. "Mr. Curran asked Pauline straight out whether she kept her room tidy or not."

"What?" cried Miss Hetty.

"He did," Stella persisted, but the Countess said:

"Hush that, Stella. It was the merest chance question, because he was laughing about his own untidy ways. And Lord knows he left his own bedroom in a mess. Papers and ashes and things strewed all over."

"I think the queerest thing," Anna said, "was that when he appeared, Pauline stared straight at him, and—she was at the coffee urn,—the cup she was filling overflowed all over the tray. You needn't tell me she had never seen him before."

"But she hadn't," the Countess averred, "she told me so herself."

"I'll tell you what," and Stella's eyes beamed with excitement, "likely as not she corresponded with him without ever having seen him! You know how girls will write to actors and authors whom they've never seen."

"Yes," cried Anna, "and she sent him her picture,—years ago,—and she didn't want Val to know about it—"

Kinney's eyes shone. He was getting what he called to himself 'great dope.' And if all these things were so,—well,—more might be so—

Angel Bob Baldwin favored the detective with an interview later.

"Don't think for a minute, Mr. Kinney," he said, "that I want to put any brake on the wheels of justice. But I do want you to beware how you manage that matter of Miss Fuller's disappearance. You know as well as I do that she never killed that man. Now, you're here to discover a murderer; not to pry into the secrets of a lady's private life. If you must interview Miss Fuller, go ahead and do it,—if you can find her. But as to raising a hue and cry over her absence, you've no right to do it."

"Leave it to me, Mr. Baldwin," said Kinney, airily. "I've learned a bit from the chatter of the women here, and I'll run this thing in my own way, if you please."

"Do; but for your own sake let it be a common-sense way. You don't want to be a laughing stock among your own colleagues, do you?"

This shaft went home, for more than once Kinney's mistakes had been a source of mirth to some.

"Well, I'll give you one bit of advice, and you can take it or leave it." Bob's tone was light, but he gave the detective a meaning look. "When you want to 'search for the woman,' don't go after an innocent and lovely lady, but find the divorced wife of Hugh Curran. Do you know anything about her?"

"No."

"Of course you don't. And she may have had nothing to do with the whole affair, but if I were a detective, the very first person I should want to interview would be the one-time Mrs. Hugh Curran."

"Mrs. Hugh Dwyer, you mean."

"Yes, of course, it would be before he took the later name. Now Mr. Kinney, take that tip for what it's worth,—but I can't help thinking that she could give you, at least, some information."

"It's a good idea, Mr. Baldwin," the detective said, slowly. "I'd have to send a man out to Reno, I suppose—"

"Well that isn't at the ends of the earth."

"No; he could make it in five days, and wire his report. A week would cover it."

"Don't do it because I say so. It's merely a suggestion. You see, Mr. Kinney, I'm a friend of Mr. Loft's and I want to do something,—anything to help him in this horrible situation."

"Yes, sir. Mr. Loft has good, staunch friends. Now, you and Mr. Knox are both racking your brains to help him,—so is Mr. Mears, for that matter,—but Mr. Mears is more interested in doing detective work himself than in doing something to help Mr. Loft. You see what I mean, sir?"

"I do, Kinney, and perhaps the efforts of Mr. Knox and myself will amount to more than young Mears' sleuthing. By the way, what is Mr. Knox doing?"

"His idea is to get more clues. As if there were any, after all these days. But he putters around in Mr. Curran's bedroom,—I mean the room he occupied in this house that night."

"Does he find anything?"

"No, sir. He pores over the book catalogues Mr. Curran had, and he mauls over the waste-basket occasionally. But he's promised not to remove or disturb anything. You never can tell when you want to check up a feather, you know."

"A feather?"

"Yes; 'feathers left around' has come to be a by-word with us,—meaning tiny clues."

"Oh, yes, I remember. Well, Kinney, if Knox finds any important feathers let me know. My deductions are often better than my discoveries."

"All right, Mr. Baldwin. And, I'll think it over, and like as not I'll try out that Reno plan."

"Do," said Angel, little dreaming what that tryout would produce!

CHAPTER 12

WITH MARY MALDEN

BY noon next day no word had been heard of Pauline. Loft called up her New York home, and inquired, guardedly, as to conditions there. He learned that Pauline's aunt was not well, and was unusually nervous. But as no definite cause was assigned for the lady's nervousness and as no undue curiosity was shown regarding Miss Fuller's movements, Loft concluded the quiet household had heard of no cause for alarm.

Without hope of much information he called up various mutual friends and also her lawyer, but he could get no hint or trace of what had become of his lost love.

Valentine Loft had ample opportunity to pursue his vaunted policy of "Do nothing and all will be done," but somehow, in this crisis the maxim seemed to him to lose its force.

He remained away from the dining-room, lunching from a tray in the library, and to him came Stella Lawrence.

"May I come in, Val, dear?" she said, trailing her scarves through the half-open door.

"I suppose so," he said, wearily; "but don't chatter about Pauline,—I can't stand it."

"No, I won't. What are you going to do about her—about finding her, I mean?"

"I'm just going to find her, that's all. I shall never give up the search and I must succeed, sooner or later."

"Val,—why do you care for her so? If any one I loved ran away from me, I shouldn't try to get them back."

"Stella, didn't you hear me ask you not to talk of Pauline?"

"No, I won't. Isn't Miss Dwyer queer, Val?"

"Yes,—she doesn't interest me. I'm very sorry for her, but she is a good deal of a nuisance about."

"And she gossips so. What do you suppose she said about Pauly?"

"I don't care to hear."

"Well, she said that Mr. Curran must have corresponded with Pauline without knowing her personally,—and she sent him her picture and all that."

"Yes?"

"Don't you care, Val? Don't you care that Pauline knew that man before, and told you she didn't? Why, it proves Pauly a naughty fibber—or should one say fibberess?"

Stella trailed across to Loft's chair, and sat on the arm of it.

"You'd better forget her, Val. I know Pauline,—truly, she isn't worthy of you. Why,—listen,—I happen to know that she was in Mr. Curran's room that night,—and that she came out of it at half-past two in the morning."

Loft reached forward and pushed a bell button.

"Go back to your seat, Stella," he said, "some one is coming."

"I don't care," and Stella remained on the chair arm.

Loft rose, and in a moment Mrs. Jennings, the housekeeper, appeared.

"Mrs. Jennings," Loft said, "Miss Lawrence is leaving on the four o'clock train. Send Tessie to help her with her packing and instruct Bates to have the little car ready."

"Yes, sir," and Mrs. Jennings went away.

"Val! How dare you? Are you driving me away? Me,—Stella?"

But Valentine Loft apparently neither saw nor heard her. He sat at a desk and began to write some letters.

One more glance at his stony profile and Stella Lawrence knew she had no choice as to her next step.

She went dejectedly from the room, her anger and indignation lost in a deeper feeling of shamed regret.

Meeting Anna in the hall she told her she had had a telegram and had to run away at once,—to another house party.

"And I'm glad to get away from this chamber of horrors," she added. "Are you staying on?"

"I don't know." Anna looked perplexed. "Now Ned says we'll go and then he stays on. We can go if we like—I mean the authorities won't keep us now."

"Then I should think you'd go," Stella said, lightly, as she trailed off to her room to do her packing.

Valentine Loft sat alone until he heard the car depart with Stella in it. Then he sent a message to the Countess asking an interview.

She came to him.

"We can be alone here," she said, gently. "You poor boy, I wish I could help you."

"Perhaps you can, Countess," he returned. "If so, it will be by utter frankness. Did you see Pauline at all the night Mr. Curran died? I mean after we had all said good-night."

Countess Galaski looked straight at him.

"You want me to tell you?"

"I do."

"Well, then, Val, it's hard to say positively, but I did see a woman in the hall that night,—who looked like Pauline. That's all I'm prepared to state."

"Please state all you know. It will help me more, Countess, to know the truth than to have my feelings spared."

"Then, Valentine, I can only say that while I am ready to state it was Pauline,—I would not be willing to swear to it. You see the difference—? Were it a casual question, I should reply, 'Yes, it was Pauline.' But if it is a weighty question, one on which other issues hang, I will not say positively."

"What made you think it was she?"

"The hall was dimly lighted, and I saw a vague figure of Pauline's height and general effect. She wore a dark gown and a cape that hung in soft folds. It was such a cape as Pauline possesses, yet that is not proof positive. Tessie could have worn that."

"Tessie is much of Pauline's figure."

"Yes,—but, Val, you asked for the truth,—it wasn't Tessie. It was a woman of the world. She carried herself as such. She walked stealthily,—but steadily,—and she went in at the door of Pauline's room."

"Having come from Hugh Curran's room?"

"That I can't say. She came from that direction,—and I heard a door close—that seemed to be his—oh, Valentine, don't make me tell these things! What do they mean?"

"That's what I must find out, Countess. They mean strange things, I've no doubt,—but they do *not* mean that Pauline is in any way implicated in the murder of Hugh Curran."

"Oh, of course not—"

"Don't say, 'oh, of course not'!" Loft's nerves were beginning to give way.

"What shall I say?" The Countess looked bewildered.

"Say you know she couldn't have been. For you do know it,—no one can help knowing it. Now I want all the information I can get about these circumstances, so I can unearth their explanation. Help me, Countess."

Beneath her dictatorial manner, Countess Galaski carried a most kind heart. She looked at Loft compassionately, and her sympathy went out to him. But her judgment told her that candor was best.

"Then I will tell you, Valentine, what I had expected to tell no one. Pauline,—for it was Pauline,—carried in her hand something that glittered. Something that might have been that watch. Only for an instant, when a straggling glint of light struck it, did I see it, and then, clasping the thing in her hand, she went into her own room."

Loft, his face stern and set, listened intently.

"Thank you, Countess," he said, after a moment's pause, "for telling me. My only desire in life is to find Pauline and tell her I love her. The watch, the picture in it,—even the distressing circumstances of Hugh Curran's death, are to me of no consequence compared to the finding of Pauline."

"And you deem her innocent?"

"Countess, I sent Stella away from the house for an aspersion on Pauline's innocence. I do not resent your speech,—only because I know you deem her innocent yourself."

"I do," she returned, and if she hadn't before, the implicit confidence Loft felt swayed her own opinion.

"There are some things to be explained," Loft admitted, "but they can be explained only by Pauline herself. And, so, until I can ask her, I put them aside. I do not speculate on their meaning."

"But, Val, you must remember, there are outsiders who do not feel as you do about it all. Who are ready to put the worst construction on Pauline's flight—"

"Of course, Countess, dear. Those are the people I have to circumvent, whose plans I have to frustrate, whose guns I must spike. And I shall do it,— why, I can do anything to save Pauline's name from the slightest stain,—to find again my darling—my love."

He almost seemed to forget the Countess' presence, as his firm, strong mouth, set in determination and a glow of lovelight came into his fine eyes.

"You're centuries behind your time, Val," she said, "you belong in the age of chivalry. You'd tourney to the death for the woman you love."

"Any real man would," he returned, "though perhaps," he looked a little whimsical, "he wouldn't say so much about it."

"I'm an old woman, Val, dear,—you may confide your feelings to me as much as you like."

"Oh, I'm not ashamed of my desperate love for Pauly,—but declarations of it naturally bore others. However, Countess, you're so delightfully understanding, that I let myself go. But, now as to this tale of yours? You know a lot about—things in general,—can you trump up any reason why Pauly should visit Hugh Curran in his room,—or why she should come away with his watch?"

"None, unless,—" she hesitated, "unless she had given him the picture long ago, in foolish flirtation,—and wanted to get it back,—and did so."

"Not good enough,"—she told me she had never seen him before. I believe her. My theory is more toward her doing it all for somebody else."

"Suppose somebody who had Pauline's picture—long ago,—gave it to Curran,—and she thought if I learned of it,—say it was Angel,—or some equally dear friend, I'd be angry at him—or maybe it was a woman—"

"Valentine, you're drivelling. You can't even voice the theory you're trying to pick out of the air. Now, stop surmising and mulling over reasons or motives and stick to facts. Where do you think Pauline is?"

"I think she is staying with some dear and true friend, who lives somewhere off the beaten paths, and that friend, sworn to secrecy, will keep Pauly in hiding as long as she wishes to be kept. It's an easy guess,—where else could she be?"

"I daresay you're right. How long will she stay there?"

"Until I can get to her,—or get a message to her to come to me."

"Would she come?"

"If she could get the message. You see, she thinks,—bless her heart,— that I'm upset over the miserable business,—and she must think that the finding of the watch in her desk has been an unpardonable sin. Silly darling! As if she could do an unpardonable thing—to me."

"Then the question of Pauline's whereabouts is at a deadlock." The Countess spoke seriously. "Do you realize what that means?"

"Lots of unpleasantness,—I'm sure. But it does not mean that she will be found—by the authorities, until she gets good and ready. It'll be all I can do to find her."

He sighed.

"How are you going to set about it?"

"Haven't the slightest idea,—yet. But an inspiration will come to me before long. You see, she's not in the vicinity of New York City at all. She's up in northern New York or in New England."

"Quite an area to search."

"Yes," he said, laconically.

* * * *

And Valentine Loft was right.

In a tiny, elm-shaded New England village, Pauline Fuller was at that moment sitting in a wicker chair on the back veranda of a pleasant country home. And she looked sadly in need of the comfort and consolation of the knowledge of her lover's faith in her.

"And so you see, Mary," she was saying, "I never want to see Val again. I couldn't hope for his forgiveness,—in his eyes it is crime,—nothing less. No power could make him understand my motive,—or see it all as I do. Oh, do you suppose they'll send out detectives after me,—and all that?"

"Don't think about it, Pauline. At least, not now. We'll have to think pretty soon,—a lot,—but today, do rest and try to calm your nerves."

"I'm not nervous," Pauline declared, "I'm only wretchedly miserable. Oh, why did I ever do it? I can't live—Mary, I can't *live* without Val!"

"Well, dear, if you get yourself all worked up, you'll have hysterics and make a lot of trouble for me. Now, get your cape, we're going for a long ride in the country. And during the ride, you're not to mention these things. Then we'll come home, have a nice cosy little dinner, and after that we'll sit down and thrash out the whole thing. You haven't told me all yet, you know."

Mary Malden, an old school friend of Pauline's mother, was a spinster, and was of the type known as salt of the earth. She had been the first one Pauline thought of in her mad flight, and she had done just exactly what Loft had surmised. She had passed three stations on the road to New York City, had left the train, turned around and retraced her path, going on up, in the region of the Berkshire hills, and had found a welcome in Mary Malden's heart and home.

The house was a small one, though comfortable, but the heart was one of the largest and kindest God ever made.

At first, Miss Malden would listen to no explanation, no word of trouble,—she only took Pauline in as a mother would take a long lost child.

And now, nearly twenty-four hours of coddling had restored Pauline's poise physically,—but her mind and soul were more perturbed than ever, and she longed for the time when Mary would listen and advise.

During the drive in Miss Malden's unpretentious little car, Pauline tried to respond to her kind friend's efforts at conversation, but it was so difficult that her hostess left her to her own thoughts,—and they were not pleasant ones.

"Why did I ever do it?" she asked herself over and over,—yet could find no answer.

"Lassitude is rather becoming to you, Pauline," Mary said, at last, in a vain hope to rouse a fleeting interest in her appearance.

"Lassitude isn't the word," Pauline tried to smile. "I'm anything but inert. I've energy enough—to—to sink a ship."

"Use it then to pull yourself together. Look here, honey, if you have a nervous collapse, or go into a decline,—or have some sort of foolish psychoneurasthenia,—or whatever the latest fad is,—I'll pack you off to a sanitarium. I can't have invalids about. People in trouble are my hobby, but people who are ill give me the creeps."

"Not a bad idea, Mary," Pauline said, "the sanitarium, I mean. Couldn't you commit me to some nice one where they keep patients in utter seclusion? Tell them I'm a little bit irresponsible, you know,—a trifle unbalanced,—and make them promise to keep it all confidential. It could be done, I'm sure."

"And it will be done, if you don't brace up and behave yourself! Moreover, I shan't stop at a sanitarium, I'll put you in an out-and-out lunatic asylum—in a straight-jacket!"

"I rather wish you would. Say, in solitary confinement,—then the police couldn't get at me!"

"The police! Good heavens, girl, is it as bad as that?"

"Yes," Pauline said, slowly, "as bad as that."

And when at last they turned homeward, when at last dinner was over and Pauline had told Mary all, all her pitiful story, Miss Malden agreed it was as bad as that.

At Valhalla, matters seemed to be at a standstill.

Detective Kinney had taken on a new and somewhat blustering manner. He dictated to everybody, except to Valentine Loft,—somehow, he couldn't quite compass that.

Angel Bob resented dictation.

"Make him stop, Val," he said, after a few days of it; "I won't be told what to do and what not to do by a whipper-snapper of a detective that can't detect a single thing!"

"There doesn't seem to be anything to detect," Loft said, with an abstracted air. "Except what has become of Pauly, and I'm going to detect that myself."

"So you've said, repeatedly. But she's been gone five days now, and you've made no headway. Can't you get busy?"

"I've laid my plans,—they're being carried out. They may work, Angel,—and, Lord help me, they may not. If not,—the case is hopeless."

"Unless Pauline returns of her own accord."

"She never will. Now, Angel, don't you stay here any longer than you wish. The police have practically released us all from surveillance,—that is, all except myself—"

"You! Since when have you been under suspicion?"

"Oh, Friend Kinney has trumped up a theory that Pauline stole the watch because it was evidence of a disgraceful past, and that I killed Curran because,—oh, I don't know why,—to wipe out the same past, I suppose."

"What rot."

"What theory isn't? Can you suggest, Angel, can you *invent* a sound theory of Hugh Curran's death? Can you imagine a motive that would fit the case or a method that would fit the facts? The police have really shelved the thing,—though they don't say so. Miss Dwyer wants to go home and I don't blame her. The Knoxes want to go,—at least, Anna does. I'm not sure about Ned,—he's so moody."

"I say, Val," Angel looked thoughtful, "you never suspected Ned,—did you?"

"No, I never did. Nor you, nor Roly, nor myself! Perhaps I'm the most likely suspect of the four, though."

"Guess we'll have to come back to old Meredith."

"As likely as anybody, I suppose. But, you didn't invent a theory."

"Tell me how a real live murderer got in and out of a locked room and I'll do the rest of the theory," Angel retorted, and the subject was dropped.

A little later, Kinney appeared, bristling with excitement and swelling with importance.

"I've had a report,—" he began, and paused; "I'd rather make it to you alone, Mr. Loft."

"Oh, go ahead," Loft returned, with little show of interest. "Mr. Baldwin is my friend, he may hear whatever you have to tell me."

"The report is from Reno," Kinney said, a little sullenly. "Shall I go ahead?"

"From Reno?" Loft cried, startled out of his usual calm by this unexpected disclosure.

"Yes, sir," Kinney said, satisfied now with the sensation he was creating. "A telegram from the man I sent out there to investigate the circumstances of Mr. Hugh Dwyer's divorce—some years ago."

"Mr. Dwyer's divorce,—has it any bearing on the case?" Loft said.

"I'll read it to you,—no, you read it yourself."

He handed over the yellow paper, and Angel noted that it was a long telegram, perhaps a night letter.

Either Valentine Loft read very slowly, or he read the screed several times, for it seemed to both Kinney and Bob that he would never raise his eyes from the typewritten lines.

Watching closely, they saw his eyes return again and again to the top and travel slowly across the lines to the bottom, only to repeat the performance.

"What is it, Val?" Baldwin asked at last, unable to stand it longer.

Loft raised his eyes then and stared at Bob, unseeing.

"Tell me, old chap," Angel persisted, longing to snatch the paper himself.

Then the two men saw such an expression of agony in the dark eyes as neither had ever before seen in mortal man.

An effort to speak proved futile; Valentine Loft was speechless.

With a sudden nervous jerk he tore the paper across and across, again and again, until it was the tiniest scraps.

"That doesn't matter," Kinney said, comfortably, "we can get duplicates from the office. It's a report copied from the Reno records of Hugh Dwyer's divorce from his wife, nearly six years ago. His wife, whom he had married about eight months previous, was Miss Pauline Fuller, of New York City. The same lady we are now trying to locate. I hope we shall be able to find her,—for more reasons than one."

CHAPTER 13

HOW LOFT TOOK IT

"I HOPE to Heaven you *will* be able to find her," said Loft, agreeing to the detective's wish, but staring at him still, with that blank, unseeing gaze. "But just now, Mr. Kinney, I'll ask you to leave me to myself for a time. You must realize that your news is a great surprise to me,—and I may have to—readjust my plans somewhat."

"Plan any way you like, Mr. Loft," Kinney said, almost cheerily, "we have enough data now to go ahead with."

"Hold on," Angel cried out, "are you sure of this tale you tell, Mr. Kinney? Don't let him 'go ahead,' Val, until we check up on this thing."

"No necessity for that, Mr. Baldwin. The agent we sent to Reno is a capable and experienced man. He would not send that definite information unless he was certain it was true. And, you must admit the circumstances all go to prove it. Here's the divorced wife of Hugh Curran—"

"Mr. Kinney, will you leave this room before I put you out?" Loft's face was menacing, his tone was desperate.

"Why, yes, Mr. Loft, I'll go. But I'm counting on finding you here when I want you. Your heroics are well done,—but, I'm not so sure you didn't know all this before, and—"

Loft suddenly jumped from his chair, his eyes blazing, and Kinney, really frightened at his approach, fled from the room.

"Angel, what does it mean?" and Valentine Loft looked despairingly at his friend.

"I don't know, Val, but it must be true. As Kinney says, such detailed and authentic information must be a statement of facts."

Loft looked up quickly, sensing a certain lack of sympathy in Baldwin's voice.

"That will do, Angel," he said, coldly, "and forgive me if I ask you to leave me alone for a bit. I've a lot to think out."

Without a word, Baldwin rose, and Loft added:

"I suppose Kinney will spread the news broadcast. That can't be helped. Do all you can for me, Angel."

"Sure," said Bob, and went on out.

Then Valentine Loft faced the situation.

At first, his mind refused to work at all. His brain was stunned, dazed, from the knowledge that had come to him.

His abhorrence of divorce was so strong,—so deep-seated in his nature, that the mere idea of connecting it with Pauline was almost impossible. Pauline,—his Pauly,—a divorced woman! And from Hugh Curran! It was incredible,—it was almost laughable! There was some mistake, of course. Another Pauline Fuller,—yes, that must be it. He would prove it,—he vowed he would prove it. That satisfied, smirking detective should eat his own words!

Loft paced up and down the room, his strides increasing in length as his mind worked itself up into a fury against the man who had dared pretend that married Pauline Fuller was his Pauly!

But rushing thoughts surged through his brain. Curiously, one of the first was the expression on Hugh Curran's face as he said to Pauline on that dreadful evening, "Are you, too, untidy about your bureau drawers, Miss Fuller?" or some such thing as that. Who but a man who had been a woman's husband would think of saying such a thing? Her husband! Pauline's husband!

Loft tore up and down the library, his brain seething, his hands clenched and his face crimson with rushing blood.

It could not be! His adored, his darling, never could have been the wife of any man! She was pledged to him,—all her sweet, girlish beauty was his own,—Curran!—divorced!

He dropped into a chair, exhausted. Slowly his face paled to a chalky white as his brain began to realize—to straighten things out, and to face the appalling truth.

It must be faced. He must understand that his Pauline had been the wife of Hugh Curran,—that she had been divorced,—and—that she had kept these facts from him.

He knew better than to doubt the truth of it all. He knew there was not the slightest hope of a mistake,—not the tiniest loophole of escape from the facts. He knew that he had to meet the situation, grapple it, wrestle with it,—and throw it,—or, be thrown!

He faced it. And as his thoughts ran riot, a dozen hints or memories came to help prove the case.

That "Rosalie" business. Miss Hetty had said that Curran called his wife Rosalie or Rosy,—though that was not her name. A nickname or pet name, then, for Pauline,—perhaps because of the rosy cheeks she had had then.

Then! Nowadays, her cheeks were always pale,—so that she indulged in a touch of rouge, sometimes.

And that evening, Curran had said: "*Rosalie*,—does that mean anything to any one here?"

And Pauline had moved restlessly,—he had seen it. And when Curran came in that day,—Pauline had let the cup she was filling overflow on the table.

Still,—Pauline had told him,—her clear eyes looking into his own, that she never had seen Hugh Curran before.

Ah,—his quick wits understood that. She never had. The man she had known was Hugh Dwyer. Curran was a new name to her.

Thinking deeply, Loft decided that Pauline did not know who Curran was until he arrived at the house.

Few knew the novelist's real name, and Loft remembered how he had jestingly described Curran's appearance in any way but the real one. Then, too, if Pauly didn't know that Dwyer had changed his name and had become an author, of course, she had no reason to suspect that the invited celebrity would turn out to be her—

Every time Loft's train of thought led him back to the awful truth,—and every time he was crushed and broken anew.

It was bad enough that Pauline had been married,—it was worse, in his eyes, that she had been divorced,—but—she had deceived him about it.

And, so,—when Curran came that day, she recognized him,—and forgot what she was pouring—and—oh, yes, he asked her to walk in the garden—alone with him. Oh, yes,—so he did.

And he had said "Rosalie,"—playing with her, as a cat with a mouse.

And he had flashed his watch open, that she might see the picture. And she did. Oh, yes.

And then—she had gone to his room,—that night—after two o'clock—well,—she had a right to—or, didn't she?

His brain raced on. She had gone to his room,—to ask for the picture,—and he—probably refused,—and then—she—his brain was working automatically now, quite independent of his mind or heart,—and then she killed him—why, of course Pauly killed him, she was the one who had advocated poison from the start.

And then she took the watch and went back to her room and hid the watch, and that meddling detective had hunted it out!

Confound him, why couldn't he leave Pauly alone?

Quite calm now, Loft went across the room to where a large silver-framed photograph of Pauline stood on a table.

He picked it up and gazed at it with a loving reverence.

"My darling," he said softly, "my blessed little girl, you are mine, and I love you—more than ever. Why did you run away from me? Didn't you know, dear heart, there is nothing I wouldn't forgive you? Nothing! Don't you know what that means? It means you can deceive me, you can commit crime, you can do anything,—and you are still my own, my Best Beloved.

"That's what love means, dear. It isn't love if it dies or even wanes because of—because of anything at all. Now, Sweetheart, my first task is to find you,—my next,—to—to take care of you and protect you.

"Where are you, Pauline? How can I get word to you? I remember how you looked,—how solemn, yes, sad, the day you told me that when you sent me just the message, 'Good-by,' it would mean good-bye forever. But it doesn't, Beloved, no, it does not! I know now what was in your mind,—this horrid old Curran business. But,—oh, my Love, didn't you know I would forgive even that? Why didn't you tell me all about it? It was my own fault, though. I denounced divorce so strongly, you thought your own pitiful little story would affect my love for you. Bless your baby heart! Six years ago you were a mere school girl. You were dragged into a marriage—well, I won't try to imagine it. When I get you back again, you shall tell me all about it while I hold you close and safe in my arms."

Loft laid his cheek against the picture for a moment and then set it back in place.

"Now," he said to himself, sitting down at the desk, "let's tabulate our procedures."

"First, I must find Pauline before those fool detectives do. Next, I must get the crowd here in the house all on Pauline's side,—or they, especially the women, will do a lot of harm. Next, I must get up some theory of Curran's death,—manufacture evidence if need be, to turn suspicion away from Pauline,—for it's bound to hit her sooner or later. Miss Dwyer will be hard to manage, I daresay. Old Angel will stand by me,—though he seemed pretty well shaken by Kinney's story—"

And then Loft's mind came back with a shock to realities.

It was all very well for him, while alone, to forgive Pauline, to rhapsodize over her portrait and to smooth her way by reason of his unalterable love,—but none of these things would help much in regard to the fearful publicity and scandal that must follow on the announcement of Kinney's report.

Well, this certainly was no occasion for his motto of "Do nothing and all will be done!" That principle would not work in this case. He must plunge in and do it all himself.

Just what he was to do, he wasn't quite sure. But he had to trust to his own wisdom and judgment to meet each phase of the situation as it presented itself, and, mentally girding his loins for battle, Loft drew himself up proudly, and went out of the library to join the others.

He found them grouped on the terrace.

He was almost amused at the various attitudes with which they greeted him.

Anna ran to him and impulsively threw her arms around his neck, crying, "I'm always your friend, Val, through thick and thin!"

Even through his preoccupied thoughts there came to Loft a sudden thought of how prone Anna was to take advantage of a situation which would give her legitimate excuse to fling her arms around a man's neck.

He gently disengaged the lovely arms, saying simply, "Thank you, Anna, I felt sure I could bank on you,—on you all," he added, looking around at them.

Baldwin nodded, Knox gave an acquiescent smile, while Roly Mears exclaimed, fervently, "You bet!"

The Countess said, very gravely, "I am your friend, Valentine,—and Pauline's."

But Miss Hetty Dwyer was plainly antagonistic.

"You can hardly expect such protestations from me, Mr. Loft," she said, icily. "I am amazed to learn that Miss Fuller is my brother's divorced wife,— though I should not be. I should have suspected at once that his reference to Rosalie was directed at her—"

"Why should it have been, Miss Dwyer?" Loft asked, quietly. "Why should your brother want to tease or annoy the woman who had been his wife?"

"Because she was playing a part! Because she was passing herself off as a girl, when she was a married woman,—a divorced woman! No discomfort he could cause her, could deeply hurt such a callous, a perverted nature—"

Valentine Loft interrupted her.

"Miss Dwyer," he said, "I want to make a statement. Miss Pauline Fuller is my fiancée, my deeply beloved bride-to-be. Nothing she has done, nothing she ever may or can do can shake my faith in her or in the slightest degree lessen my love for her. Now, then: no one under my roof may make the least unpleasant allusion to her, or say the merest word of reproach or unkindness. This understood, you are all welcome to the hospitality of my home as long as you choose to stay here. I shall be glad of your company, but I will not tolerate a word, a hint or a look that is unfriendly to Pauline Fuller. Am I clear?"

"You are, Val, and I heartily stand by you," declared Knox, and Baldwin murmured, "Me, too."

"But, Valentine," Roly Mears exclaimed, "we've got to look into these matters. We can't just sit down and do nothing. And, who knows where the investigation may lead?"

Loft smiled a little.

"Roly," he said, "I'm not thinking of you. You go ahead with your 'investigation,' perhaps you'll be of real help. Countess, where do you stand?"

"At your side, Val. Count on me for love and sympathy with Pauline, and you must forgive me if I go so far as to say, that I shall love her just the same through good report and evil report."

"Thank you, Countess, I take that exactly as I know you mean it. Now, we are all in accord,—except, perhaps, Miss Dwyer."

"Indeed you may except me,—I have no feelings in accord with those who would protect the murderess of my brother. I have no sympathy for a woman who could deceive the man who loved and trusted her, who could pretend she was an unmarried woman, when—"

"I don't think you need go over that again, Miss Dwyer," Loft spoke evenly; "will it not do if you merely say you do not care to stay with us, and make your adieux?"

"I have no intention of doing anything of the sort, Mr. Loft," the spinster retorted. "I am here, and here I stay until the mystery of my brother's death is solved. Of course, if you ask me to leave your house, I shall do so, but I shall stay in the vicinity."

"You are welcome to stay in my house, Miss Dwyer, as long as it suits your convenience, on the sole condition that you speak no word of unpleasant import concerning Miss Fuller. You may think what you choose, but I must insist that under my roof no hint of disparagement of her shall be voiced. I have your promise?"

"Yes. When I feel that I can no longer hold my tongue, I shall go away."

"Very well, then," and Valentine Loft turned from the lady, as one who has no further interest.

There was a somewhat embarrassing silence after that. Every one of his guests was anxious to talk to Loft alone, but none seemed to care about joining in a general conversation.

Moreover, no one knew exactly what to say.

But Loft gave no opportunity for desultory chatter.

"You fellows come with me, will you?" he said, and led the way back to the library.

Baldwin, Knox and Roly Mears followed him, leaving the women to pursue their own vocations.

"Now, here's the situation," Loft said, in his most business-like manner, "Pauline is the divorced wife of Hugh Curran,—or Hugh Dwyer, as he was then. She has run away because she thinks I would be so shocked at the knowledge of this that I would care less for her. As a matter of fact the knowledge in no way affects my attitude toward her, and, naturally I want her to know that as soon as possible. But, with all my desire to do so, I cannot find her at once. I hope to do so, but I know it will be a difficult task. Now, meanwhile, the police, with their widespread detective facilities, may succeed in finding her before I can do so. They follow up a disappearance by means of their scattered agents, and I am alone in my search?"

"Let me help you, Val," said Mears, eagerly. "I can trace her—"

"All right, Roly, go ahead. But your success is, to say the least, problematical; and I'm alarmed for another reason. To put it plainly, boys, it is almost inevitable that Pauline should be suspected of killing Hugh Curran. Kinney is sure of it, and if he can find her she will be arrested at once. This you can all see is an imminent danger. It must be averted. So, I propose to give myself up for the murder of Curran."

"You!" Baldwin stared at him.

"Yes. I say now to you all that I killed Hugh Curran that night."

"The only trouble is," Knox put in, "nobody will believe you."

"That's just it. And that's where I count on you fellows to help me out. If I go to the police and give myself up, they will say, 'No, you are merely doing that to shield Miss Fuller.' So, I want one of you to go to Kinney and tell him convincingly,—convincingly, mind you,—that you suspect me. You can say my motive was to keep Miss Fuller's secret from becoming public property. Or say I killed him in a fit of jealous rage,—we'll make up the best and most plausible story we can,—but it must be a good one. Who'll do this? You, Angel?"

"No, Val, I can't. Don't ask me to. I'm no good at that wool-pulling stunt,—I wish I could,—but, oh, hang it all, old man,—I just can't!"

Angel's blue eyes showed deep distress, and his face was drawn with anxiety and apprehension. He averted his gaze from Loft, and said, "It's a fool plan,—you can't put it over."

Roly looked amazed.

"If you do put it over," he said, "they'll take you at your word,—and hang you!"

"I doubt it," Loft returned, "but I'll take that chance. Will you do it for me, Ned?"

"Not without thinking it over first. And, I say, Val, suppose you're arrested, and Pauline hears of it,—which, of course, she would, she'll come flying back to confess herself,—if she did it."

"She never did it," Loft said, stubbornly. "Get that in your heads, all of you. But she's going to be suspected—accused of it,—and I've got to save her! I can't think of any other way,—so, I *did* do it."

"How'd you work it?" Baldwin asked. "How'd you lock the door after you?"

"I had a sort of skeleton key, that turns the door key from the other side."

"Can't be done."

"I did it," and Loft's calm serenity made it almost seem as if he were stating a fact instead of playing a rôle. "I'd ask you to do this thing for me, Roly, but—well, I know you'd muff it. Angel or Ned could pull it off,—but you couldn't. You can help, though, corroborate, you know."

"Oh, I can't bring myself to try it on, Val," Knox looked sorry. "Really, old man, it wouldn't carry through."

"That's my business," and Loft set his lips stubbornly. "Well, if you won't, then I shall have to go and give myself up,—but I know it would be twice as convincing if *you'd* carry the message to Garcia. I can vow I did it,—and—well, perhaps I can make it realistic enough to fool those purblind police. So you all refuse?"

"I do," Baldwin said, decidedly. "And I'm against it. You'll get nowhere,—and, have you thought of this? When the police hear your confession, and know,—as they will,—that you're inventing it to save Pauline,—they'll realize your fear of her guilt and they'll be surer than ever of it."

Loft looked at him contemplatively.

"You don't think Pauly did it, Bob?"

"I do not. But the police will be sure of it if you go in for that fool quixotic scheme you propose."

"I don't know about that. I'll mull it over some more and see. Roly, sometimes you have brilliant ideas,—what do you suggest?"

"I'll tell you what I suggest," and Roly looked very earnest. "I know you all think I'm awful young and don't know anything about real detecting. And I guess you're right, I don't. Not in a big thing like this. But, I'm positively sure that there's a greater mystery here than we know about yet. And I know those dunder-headed police will never find it out. So I propose, Val, that you get Fleming Stone, the detective."

"Never heard of him."

"Well, he's well known among people who have had reason to employ him."

"One of those story-book detectives?" Angel asked, with a smile.

"Well, he's deductive and all that,—but he's got a lot of good sound common sense, too. Anyway, he'll find Pauline, and he'll find out the truth."

"Do you want the truth found out, Val?" and Angel looked at Loft closely.

"Yes, I do," he said, after a moment's pause. "Pauline never killed that man,—but if she did,—there was good reason,—and she'll be exonerated. Mind you, I say she didn't,—but I also say I'm ready to face the truth,—and if she did,—she is still my Pauline."

"Good for you," cried Roly, "you're the real thing, Val. Will you send for Stone,—or shall I?"

"You can do it, Roly, if you will. But let me see him first when he arrives."

CHAPTER 14

FIBSY MEETS A COUNTESS

AS the car rolled smoothly up the long drive through the tree-shaded lawns of Valhalla, Fleming Stone and his able assistant, young McGuire, gazed in silent admiration at the beautiful well-kept place.

"When I have made my world-wide reputation, F. Stone," the boy said, "and have solved my last case, I shall retire on my income and live in just such a place as this."

"Last week you planned a castle on the Palisades,—and the month before, you thought you'd like a California villa."

"All off,—this is the sort of thing for an American gentleman,—which I shall be by then."

Stone forbore to smile at the freckled-faced, red-haired lad in the rôle of a country gentleman, but he gave him a sympathizing look and said, "I hope you'll realize some one of your air castles, Fibsy."

"Yessir. What do you know about this present disturbance, F. Stone?" he asked, as they came in sight of the house.

"Only the main facts. But it's the always interesting question of the victim in a locked room——"

"And a beautiful lady. When I'm in this business for myself, F. S., I shall take only cases that include the beautiful lady."

"But in this case, the lady has disappeared."

"That's the beauty of it. I shall have the pleasure of finding her. Won't that be nice?"

"Very nice, Terence, and I hope you may do so. To me this whole case is a bit serious."

"Then it is to me, too, F. Stone," and the freckled face at once became grave.

Terence McGuire was Irish, and therefore possessed of quick wits and a warm heart. Both these attributes were dedicated to the service of Fleming Stone, and as the years went by, Stone depended more and more on his young assistant, who was rapidly becoming a colleague.

When taking a case, Stone acquainted himself, if possible, with the principal facts and conditions, but kept an open mind as to deductions therefrom, until he could see and hear details on the scene itself.

The pair were received in the library by Valentine Loft alone.

"The case is a peculiar one, Mr. Stone," he opened the subject; "and I'm not sure you will want to conduct it as I wish. If not, just say so. I am employing you,—your reports are due to me only. While in no conflict with the police, at the same time I do not propose to take them into my confidence unless I choose to do so."

"May I anticipate your intentions, Mr. Loft, by asking if yours is not the attitude of one who wishes my services in so far as they result in accordance with your desires,—and,—no further?"

Loft was a little taken aback at this perspicacity, but he said, frankly, "that is not far from the truth, Mr. Stone. But I hope,—I am trusting that there will be no conflict between your discoveries and my inclinations."

"Put it more plainly," Stone said, briefly.

"Very well. My fiancée, Miss Pauline Fuller, has disappeared. This fact has caused the police to suspect her of the murder of Mr. Curran. You know the circumstances of his death?"

"Yes, in the main. Go on."

"Miss Fuller has been proved to be the divorced wife of Mr. Curran, and, the police assume, she killed him in order to protect her secret, or because of some unknown reason connected with their married life. I'm speaking very plainly, for I want to insist that there shall be no secrets between you and me. Now, here's my position. If Miss Fuller is innocent, I want it proved. If she is guilty, I want the fact concealed and her innocence falsely proved. Do you see?"

"I see."

"This proposal could not be made to a guardian of the law, a dispenser of justice,—but a detective is not necessarily that. It is not only to find out the truth that I ask you, it is to prove to the public the innocence of Miss Fuller, whether she be innocent or not."

"Is she innocent?"

"I believe she is,—but, of course, I should believe that, unless she herself should tell me the contrary. But do your very best to prove her innocent, and if you cannot do so, then do your very best to cover her guilt from the public eyes."

"I suppose you know you are asking me to compound a felony."

"You are entirely at liberty to refuse to take the case at all."

"But I shall take it, Mr. Loft, and I am taking it because I want to discover the truth for myself. I certainly cannot promise to conceal the fact, if I find Miss Fuller guilty, but I will agree to tell you first,—and you may take what steps you choose."

"And you?"

"I shall be guided entirely by circumstances. I bind myself by no promises,—but I think I shall not disappoint you. There may be other directions in which I look than toward Miss Fuller. The case seems to me to present a number of angles."

"Is there any one you suspect, Mr. Loft?"

The question came from Fibsy, who sat, looking earnestly at the master of the house.

Loft looked at the lad a little surprised, for he had thought him a mere clerical assistant of the detective, or, perhaps, errand boy.

But the clear gaze of the blue eyes held his attention, and Loft replied, thoughtfully, "No, I can't say that I have. You see, no one I know could have any motive,—that I can think of. So, I think—I hope, the murderer was some one I never heard of. Of course, Curran was a stranger to us all—except Miss Fuller."

The pain that showed in Loft's eyes was so poignant that Fibsy turned away his head. The boy was sympathetic to a degree, and he vowed to himself that he would work hard on the case and do all he could in Loft's interests, whatever the result.

"Well, Mr. Loft," Stone finally summed up, after some few general questions, "I will begin my investigations at once. I've no wish to work incognito or to keep my presence here a secret, as I sometimes have occasion to do. I'd like to mingle with your household, chat with the guests, interview the servants, discuss matters with the local police,—if they are willing,—and generally inform myself on the situation, making what deductions I may as I go along."

Stone looked so capable, so efficient, that Loft felt encouraged.

"Very well, Mr. Stone," he agreed. "I'll have you and Mr. McGuire shown to your rooms, and as soon as you like, we will call a conclave of the people."

"Are all here who were here at the time of Mr. Curran's death?"

"No; three have left. But I think you may feel sure they were in no way connected with the crime."

"If it was a crime," Stone added, "may it not have been an accident?"

Loft's face brightened. "We've never thought of that," he cried. "We've discussed suicide and murder, but accident never occurred to us."

"Can it," said Fibsy, seriously. "It couldn't have been accident. Where'd the poison come from for accidental use?"

Loft's face fell. Already he had come to look on the boy's opinions with thoughtful attention. It mattered not to him that McGuire was a young, half-grown chap, or that his words were not chosen from the most elegant English. There was something in Fibsy's face and manner that appealed to Valentine Loft's sense of reality, and he readily listened when the boy talked. And so, his quick turndown of the accident theory made Loft see at once that it really was untenable.

Stone and Fibsy were given adjoining rooms, and as they had rather a long confab as soon as they were alone, it was luncheon time before they saw Loft again.

Then introductions were general and the party adjourned to the dining-room.

By experience in connection with Stone's cases, Fibsy had learned the principles of etiquette, at least, sufficiently to make a presentable appearance at a well-ordered table.

He was about to take the chair Loft designated for him, when the Countess exclaimed: "You funny boy! Come right over here by me. Roly, you take that other seat."

A glance at Stone, who nodded, and then Fibsy obediently went over and seated himself beside the Countess.

He was quite alive to the fact that, for the first time in his life he was seated next a titled person, and he greatly enjoyed it, though outwardly careless of the honor.

"Why are you called Fibsy?" the Countess inquired bluntly.

"Because I tell fibs, madam," he returned, wondering if he ought to say, "Your Grace," and concluding to ask Stone about it later.

"Indeed! And why do you tell fibs?"

"Because of necessity, madam; I only tell them when it is best and wisest to do so."

"You seem to be a remarkable child!"

"Yes, madam,—I am."

"And conceited!"

"No, if you please. The remarkable thing about me is that I have gained the friendship of Mr. Fleming Stone,—and that I am able to make myself useful to him."

"You are fond of him?"

"Oh, gee! yes! I beg your pardon, madam, but added to my untruthfulness I am possessed of a sad addiction to slang phrases."

"You are simply delicious!" the Countess exclaimed; "I've never met any one more refreshing!"

"Pleased to meet you," said Fibsy, and rolled his blue eyes at her so comically that she shook with laughter.

Always quick to discern those who could be of help to him, especially among the women, Fibsy had picked out the Countess and Anna Knox as being the most promising.

Miss Dwyer he shrank from at once. Greatly alive to personalities, Fibsy had no use for the spinster, he concluded.

Nor did she seem to have any for him. She glared at him as at an intruder, and though she didn't say outright that he had no right to be at the family table, she hinted as much, and Loft was obliged to resent it.

"I reserve the privilege of ordering my household appointments," he said, with a frowning glance at her, and she subsided, though not without a scornful look at Fibsy.

After luncheon they gathered on the veranda, and Fleming Stone began at once to ask questions.

His manner was grave, his speech cultured and refined, and his hearers were all impressed with the kindness of his demeanor and the gentle quality of his character.

Yet as his shrewd eyes roved from one face to another, Fleming Stone gathered a good deal more than met the ear.

His inquiries brought out not only the facts as they were known, but the interpretations the various minds put upon them.

Miss Dwyer was loquacious; and as she was, in a way, most concerned with the dead man, Loft let her talk all she chose.

And it was in her account of the discussion of ways and means of murder that Stone showed his first decided interest.

He asked over just which methods were selected by the different men, and then Miss Dwyer said, spitefully, "and it was Miss Fuller herself who chose poison as the medium!"

"That seems to be a point in her favor," Stone said, thoughtfully. "I should say if any one of the people who discussed the matter should turn out to be the murderer, he or she would use a means other than the one of which they, personally, expressed approval."

"Exactly," agreed Loft, delighted at any hint in favor of Pauline.

"After methods, let's consider motives," Stone went on, suavely, but with a carefully veiled scrutiny of the faces before him.

Fibsy, too, under cover of a disinterested nonchalance was taking his cue from Stone, and watching the countenances of all present.

"I can't imagine any motive on the part of any one present," Loft declared, "unless it be myself. You might say, that if I knew or suspected Curran's previous relationship to—to Miss Fuller, I might have killed him in a fit of angry passion."

"However, we know you didn't," Ned Knox said, "so why waste time on that?"

"I'm not so sure he didn't," Miss Dwyer said, with asperity. "To me it seems quite possible that Mr. Loft did know about it and perhaps surprised the pair together in Mr. Curran's room, and so he killed him."

"There seems to have been little or no opportunity for that," Stone said. "As I see it, whoever killed Mr. Curran did so in a most clever and ingenious way. To administer prussic acid, and leave no trace of the method or manner of its administering, is to my mind the work of a diabolically clever brain."

"Yes, I agree to that," said Angel, thoughtfully.

"But," Stone went on, "I have a belief that the smarter the criminal the easier he is to catch."

"That's a strange theory," Knox said, surprised.

"But true. Your stupid dolt, who kills on an impulse, is often harder to apprehend than the smart Aleck who takes pains to hide his clues."

"And leave no feathers around," put in Loft.

And as Stone looked inquiringly, he related the story of the negro and the stolen chickens.

Fibsy laughed outright.

"That's a good one," he said. "Feathers left around! And F. Stone can take those feathers and construct the whole bird,—just like the Natural History guys do."

"Next," Stone went on, "what about alibis? Don't think I'm accusing any member of the household,—but I must check up your whereabouts that night."

He listened to their stories, and summed up thus:

"Then, Mr. and Mrs. Knox were in separate rooms, with a bathroom and two closed doors between. Mr. and Mrs. Meredith were in one room. Miss Lawrence, Miss Fuller and Countess Galaski, each in a room by herself. Mr. Loft and Mr. Baldwin, in two adjoining rooms, only one of which, Mr. Loft's, opened on the hall. And Mr. Mears in a room alone. Now, as you must see, with the possible exception of Mr. Baldwin and the Merediths, no one has a real alibi. Any one could have gone into the hall, into Mr. Curran's room, and back again, without necessarily arousing any one else."

"Did any one see or hear any such occurrence?"

"I did," said the Countess, "and I propose to tell of it, for it will come out, and I can give the unvarnished truth. Others might exaggerate or garble it. I saw Miss Fuller come out of Mr. Curran's room that night sometime after two o'clock. She carried with her something that shone and glittered,—and which, I have no doubt, was Mr. Curran's watch,—with her picture in it. I am telling this because it seems to be in Miss Fuller's favor. She never killed that man! If she had done so, she would, as Mr. Stone says, have used any means other than poison. But she didn't do it, because it is not in Pauline Fuller's nature to commit crime. And, too, why should she kill him? She was divorced from him,—what had she to fear from him?"

"Countess," Bob Baldwin said, "you think you are doing a wise thing to talk like that of Pauline,—but I advise you to stop. We, who know and love her, feel how impossible it is that she could have committed crime,—but others,—strangers,—may not judge her so leniently or so truly."

"That's so, Countess," Loft said. He had been dumfounded by the Countess' speech, and he wished, uneasily, that she would stop talking like that.

"Now, don't be alarmed about Mr. Stone and me making any mistakes in judging the lady in question," Fibsy said, suddenly.

His eyes were shining, and his shock of red hair was rumpled where he had unconsciously pulled at it, in his deep absorption in the recital of the Countess.

"In fact," Fibsy went on, "I may say, that I noted in Madam Countess' story a pretty strong indication that Miss Fuller certainly did *not* kill Mr. Curran."

"Bless you, boy!" the Countess exclaimed. "I wonder if you mean that."

"Yes, I do," Fibsy declared, "though I may be mistaken. We're not infallible,—F. Stone and me."

"May I inquire, Mr. Stone," said Miss Dwyer, acidly, "if that boy is head of your firm, or if you are?"

"It isn't a firm," Stone returned, a quiet smile on his face. "McGuire is my valued assistant, that is all. His quick wits and young eyes sometimes discern things that I myself should not have noticed."

"Oh, come now," and Fibsy looked bashful, "that ain't quite right. Only I pick up now and then some feathers left around, that Mr. Stone hasn't time to stoop for."

"You're a darling!" the Countess cried, enthusiastically, "and I shall leave you something in my will."

"No time like the present," murmured Fibsy, with a saucy glance that delighted the old lady.

"At any rate, I shall address myself only to you, Mr. Stone," Miss Dwyer went on. "Have you any idea, as yet, who killed my brother? Do you expect to find out? How soon do you expect to do so? Have you made any real progress during this inquiry you have just been holding? Do you really think that because these men talked over detective methods or murder methods with my brother, who was a writer of such stories, that there is the slightest reason to suspect one of them? Are you really trying to solve the mystery of my brother's death,—or, are you only trying to exonerate from suspicion Miss Pauline Fuller—as she calls herself?"

With difficulty Valentine Loft restrained his angry retort to this harangue, but Stone had already taken the lead.

"Miss Dwyer," he said, pleasantly, but with an undertone of sternness, "I find it difficult to remember all your queries. But I will say that I am searching for the truth and the truth only. I do not think that because a man talks over methods of murder he is necessarily himself a criminal. I have made real progress in my quest during this present session, and while I have not yet a definite idea of the name of your brother's murderer, yet I have made steps toward that, by eliminating one or two possible suspects. May I ask you in future to ask me questions in smaller quantities at a time?"

"You're a queer detective," Miss Dwyer vouchsafed.

"You are," Little Anna agreed. She had begun to feel less awe of Stone and her innate desire to receive attention made it impossible to keep silent longer. "I thought detectives asked a line of questions just as fast as they could talk."

"We do, sometimes," Stone smiled at her. Few could help smiling at Little Anna. "But a rightminded detective questions different people differently. When I tackle the servants of this establishment, I shall doubtless ask them a line of questions. But among us,—as equally intelligent people, I prefer to get at what I want by desultory chat. Besides, it's pleasanter."

"What were those things Mr. Curran said, when he pretended to be mind reading?" Fibsy asked. "I heard you mention them at luncheon, but didn't get them all."

"I'll tell you," said the Countess, beaming kindly on her new favorite. "He told me that he could read in my mind that my shoes were too tight. He was absolutely correct, but as my face was all screwed up with pain, it didn't show very desperate clairvoyant powers."

"What else?" asked Fibsy, and Stone listened, too.

"Why, he spoke of *Rosalie* and asked if it meant anything to anybody. Of course, we know now, it meant a lot to Pauline,—poor child. Then, Mr. Curran spoke of a *Mr. S.*, who, of course, was also some man of whom Pauline knew, and whom doubtless, she preferred not to remember. As I see it now, he was merely baiting Pauline all the while."

"Yes?" said Stone. "Do you know who this *Mr. S.* could have been, Miss Dwyer?"

"I do not. I haven't the slightest idea. I suppose it was some man his wife had—"

Stone interrupted her, and went on, placidly: "And, I am told, Mr. Curran collected old and rare books?"

"Yes," Loft replied, for Miss Dwyer was silently sulking. "Mr. Baldwin here can tell you the details of that matter. He is a connoisseur."

"Ah, yes; I collect some myself." Stone smiled at Angel. "Perhaps we can do a browse in the Loft library, Mr. Baldwin."

"At your service," said Bob, but he seemed disinterested, as he oftenest was, when amateurs wanted to consult with him.

And then in his courteous way, Stone implied the confab was over for the moment, and he went away to interview the servants.

CHAPTER 15

THE NEEDLE AGAIN

FLEMING STONE stood on the veranda waiting for the car which was to take him to see Doctor Gilvray. Fibsy stood beside him, quiet of manner but with his quick-darting eyes taking in everything about him.

Roly Mears approached the detective a little diffidently.

"Mr. Stone," he said, "would you mind if I went with you to the doctor's?"

"Not at all, Mr. Mears, come along."

Greatly pleased at Stone's affability, and hoping to learn some of his conclusions, Roly went along.

"I don't want to be intrusive," he said, on the way, "but have you come to any decisions, Mr. Stone?"

"A difficult question to answer," Stone said, smiling. "I've come to several decisions, but to no conclusion."

"I don't know the difference," Roly said, honestly, his face rather blank.

"Well, then, I've decided that I must first find out what killed Mr. Curran. That's a decision, and I hope it will lead to a conclusion on that subject."

"But, we know it was prussic acid."

"Yes, but I mean how administered, in what form and by what method!"

And then they were at the doctor's, who received them in his private office. He looked dubiously at Fibsy, but learning that he belonged with Stone, he seemed satisfied.

"Now, Doctor Gilvray," Stone said, as they discussed the case, "how many ways are there of administering that particular poison?"

"It may be swallowed or it may be inserted into the flesh," the doctor returned. "In this case we have to assume swallowing, because a distinct odor was noticed on the dead man's lips. The absence of any trace of poison in the stomach, merely proves that there was only a minute quantity taken."

"A minute quantity is enough to produce death?"

"Oh, yes,—the merest speck."

"Instantaneously?"

"Practically so; an interval of a very few minutes might elapse before the victim ceased to breathe."

"Can you explain the fact that there were traces in the mouth but not in the stomach,—even granting a minute portion of the acid?"

"No, Mr. Stone,—not to my own entire satisfaction. I can only say it was the poison that caused Mr. Curran's death."

"What is its exact action?"

"It is an active paralyzant and exerts a lethal influence over every part of the body. The nervous system, heart, respiratory organs, brain, and all vital parts are killed at once. The victim dies, with a gasp. For an instant the face is convulsed, the eyes wide open, teeth clenched,—all these symptoms were present in Mr. Curran's case."

"How are you so certain there was no poison in the stomach?"

"Because at an autopsy, in such cases, there is a fleeting but unmistakable odor of bitter almonds when the body is opened. There was none,—of that I am positive."

"Haven't you omitted the suggestion that the poison might have been taken by inhalation—of fumes?"

"It may be so taken, but as there was no evidence of any such possibility, I elided it."

"Yet there was no evidence of the presence of the poison in powder or in liquid form."

"True." Doctor Gilvray looked so puzzled and distressed that Stone ceased to question him. The old physician was clearly at his wits' end to account for the circumstances of the case.

"You know," Roly Mears said, "that night as Ned Knox passed the door of Mr. Curran's room, when Angel was in there with him, Ned heard them saying something about a needle. I've thought it might have been a hypodermic needle,—maybe Curran had suicidal intent and maybe Bob was trying to dissuade him."

Stone looked up quickly.

"More likely," he said, "if they really were talking of a hypodermic needle, or, of poisoning at all, more likely they were still discussing Curran's detective stories. We have no suspicions of Mr. Baldwin, have we? And, too, if he planned to kill Mr. Curran by means of a hypodermic, he would scarcely be chatting it over with him. Do you remember what Mr. Knox overheard, exactly?"

"No," Roly said, "but it was about the needle. The needle was the point at issue, of that Knox is certain. I've talked to him a lot about it. He gathered that Curran had the needle himself."

"And that Mr. Baldwin wanted it?"

"I don't know about that. You see, Ned thought nothing of it, except that a needle was a queer thing to be discussing so earnestly."

"Were the men angry?"

"Not at all, Knox says. But Curran was talking loudly, and Angel was not."

"Well, I can't see how Mr. Curran could have been killed by a hypodermic needle at that early hour, since he was seen alive later, by Mrs. Knox, by the maid, Tessie, and,—as we are told,—by Miss Fuller. By that time, Mr. Baldwin was tucked away in Mr. Loft's bedroom."

"Much as I hate to say so, I can't see any real suspect but Miss Fuller," Doctor Gilvray said, and his sad face told how he grieved at the thought.

"It looks that way, but I will not believe it," Mears declared.

"If it looks that way, we must look that way," Stone said, gravely.

"And p'raps," Fibsy said, "if *we* look that way, maybe we can stop *its* looking that way."

"Perhaps," Stone agreed. "And, now, Doctor Gilvray, it will be necessary that I shall see the body of Mr. Curran. Can you arrange that for me?"

"Yes,—Mr. Stone,—" the doctor hesitated, "if you are sure it is necessary."

"I am sure," Stone said. "Otherwise, I can never arrive at the truth of this thing. No disparagement whatever, Doctor, to your report of the autopsy,—that is clear and correct. But I must examine that body."

"Very well," the doctor replied, and promised to make the desired arrangements.

Returning to Valhalla, Fleming Stone asked for an interview with Loft, in which he inquired very definitely concerning the knowledge and the discoveries Loft might have made of Miss Fuller's present abiding place.

"I have no knowledge whatever," Loft said, dismally. "I am utterly at a loss to imagine where she is, but, knowing her as I do, I am sure she is safely hidden from detectives or from myself."

"It's not easy to hide so completely," Stone said.

"No; but it's possible," Loft returned. "You must know, yourself, Mr. Stone, that a man mightn't do it, but a woman can retire to some inconspicuous spot, and remain there undiscovered for a long time."

"That's true," Stone said; "but how does Miss Fuller get money,—how get in touch with her aunt, if necessary,—in a word, how does she communicate with the outside world?"

"She doesn't," Loft replied, gloomily. "You see, Miss Fuller has a wide circle of devoted friends. I could name half a dozen who would willingly, gladly give her sanctuary, no matter what she may have done. These friends would be wise enough and clever enough to keep her presence safely hidden from any prying detectives or inquisitors. It would not be so difficult. Imagine a large country house, with lots of guests coming and going,—or, better, imagine a small country home, on the outskirts, say, of some tiny village, or farther out in the country. Granted a determined hostess, Miss Fuller could be an unsuspected guest, indefinitely. At any rate, Mr. Stone, I am positive that is where Miss Fuller is,—at some such place."

"You've tried to communicate with her?"

"I have sent letters to her in care of five such homes as I've just mentioned, but they were all returned with the statement that she was not there. But that doesn't shake my belief. Either the people were untruthful, out of loyalty to her, or she is at some other place."

Fibsy looked deeply thoughtful.

"Do you think she may be in some farmhouse, or some small house in the country, Mr. Loft?" he asked earnestly.

"It may well be," Loft replied. "That's where I picture her. But I shall write no more letters, she will not let them be answered."

"And you can get no information from Miss Fuller's home in New York?" Stone asked.

"No. You see, Miss Fuller is very much alone in the world. Her aunt who lives with her in her city home, is a nervous invalid, and pays no attention to her niece's comings or goings. I have learned that she thinks Miss Fuller is still here, and I have not undeceived her. I have found out, too, that Miss Fuller's lawyer does not know where she is,—that is, he says he doesn't,— and her bankers profess the same ignorance. Now, it's quite possible that these people do know, but deny the knowledge, holding it as a business secret. At any rate, I cannot find out. You see, Miss Fuller can get money from her friends without trouble."

"As you put it, the whole affair is plausible enough from the very fact that it is so casual," Stone said, after a moment's thought. "True, a man,— especially a business man,—would find it difficult to drop out of existence, but a woman,—and a desperate woman, can do many seemingly impossible things."

"Say, Mr. Loft," Fibsy put in, "you think maybe Miss Fuller is at a farmhouse,—where?"

"Probably up in Connecticut,—or Massachusetts. She has many friends in all parts of the Berkshire regions. Also in New Jersey. And in the Southern States,—but I think she is not very far away."

"You're basing your assumptions on your intimate knowledge of Miss Fuller's mind?" Stone asked.

"Exactly that," Loft replied. "I know her indomitable will, I know that she has disappeared without a word; she proposes to stay hidden, but I also know, Mr. Stone, that she never killed that man!"

"I wish your conviction were positive proof," Stone said, gravely.

"I wish so, too," Loft agreed. "But I can't expect those who do not know Miss Fuller as I do, to realize the depths of her nature. I appreciate, Mr. Stone, as you cannot, the motives that led to her deception of myself. It was, primarily my own fault. I had no right to be so arbitrary in my denunciation of divorce. It was, I see now, merely a whim of mine, and had I not given way to it, Pauline might have confessed all to me. I am thus frank with you, because I want you to understand the situation perfectly."

"I think I do, Mr. Loft," Stone spoke sympathetically.

"I know I do," Fibsy said, eagerly,—"and what's more, Mr. Loft, I have a notion I can find Miss Fuller for you."

"Good boy!" Loft said, in a kindly way, but in a tone which showed clearly he had small hope of Fibsy's making good his promise.

But the boy wagged his head sagaciously, and Stone could see that some ingenious scheme had sprouted in his fertile brain.

"What's the big idea, Fibs?" he asked, when the two were later alone in Stone's room.

"I haven't quite doped it out yet, Mr. Stone," and Fibsy's blue eyes looked deep with anxiety. "But I have a glimmering of a notion—aw, shucks,—wait till I give it another think, then I'll tell you."

"All right, McGuire. Now, how about giving Mr. Curran's room a sweeping glance?"

"Let's," and the boy jumped up readily.

So to the locked room the two went, and Stone producing the key Loft had given him, they went in and locked the door behind them.

"Very few feathers left around," Stone said, somewhat chagrined at the slight effect of personal occupancy the room presented.

"Mr. Loft said nothing has been touched," Fibsy reminded him. "Surely you can find something indicative, F. S."

"Let's hope so."

Stone scanned in turn each article of furniture, the walls, the floor, the window sills and door frames.

"Not much," he concluded. "How about the waste-basket,—turn it out, Fibs."

On an outspread newspaper, Fibsy emptied the basket.

Attentively the detective scanned the motley array of rubbish.

"Most wastebaskets speak louder than this one," he said, grimly. "Can you hear anything, Fibs?"

"Nope," and the boy looked hopelessly at some torn papers, some bits of string, some lead pencil shavings, an empty cigarette box, an empty box that had evidently held digestive tablets, a wooden toothpick, a quill toothpick, a torn toothpick paper, a few burnt matches, and an old envelope or two.

Nearly all these things were duplicated on the floor of the room, proving a most careless occupant, and also proving, that as Loft had said, nothing had been disturbed.

"That medicine box might have held the poison," Fibsy said, half-heartedly, "but it doesn't look that way to me."

"No;" and Stone smelled of the pasteboard carton. "I doubt it."

But he picked out two or three of the articles from the waste-basket rubbish and put them in his note-book for future study.

"You see, the windows are fastened securely, with six-inch openings for ventilation," Fibsy remarked, and Stone said, "Yes," disinterestedly.

"And, I say, F. Stone, this door, if locked, never could be opened from the outside,—you can see that."

"Yes, I see that."

"Then how in the name of Emile Gaboriau did the murderer get in and out?"

"Be more meticulous, Terence. You mean how did he get out? He could get in easily enough."

"Curran let him in?"

"Surely."

"And then he accomplished his fell purpose?"

"He did."

"And then, how did he get out?"

"Curran let him out."

"While he was dead?"

"No,—alive."

"But, the doctor said his death was instantaneous."

"Yes,—oh, hush up, Fibsy! This is a wonderful case! But I can't be certain about it until I have seen the body of Hugh Curran."

"Say, F. Stone, it wasn't the Pauline lady,—was it?"

"It may have been,—so far we've found no one else with a motive."

"Oh,—I can't believe it—that lovely lady!"

"McGuire, you'll never make a detective unless you are willing to seek the woman. If you start out on the premise of a man miscreant always, you'll get nowhere,—you'll get sadly left."

"Well,—I'm starting out this trip with the premise that Miss Fuller is as innocent as they make 'em, and therefore I'm going to produce her and let her state her innocence for herself. She can put up the goods."

"Just how are you going to find her, Fibs?"

And then, in a few words, McGuire detailed his plan.

"Good enough in theory," was Stone's comment, "but extremely dubious in practice. However, go ahead,—if Loft agrees."

And then Stone was called downstairs to meet Detective Kinney who greatly desired to see him.

Fibsy went along, his head full of his own scheme of things.

So engrossed was he in his plans, that he paid little attention to the conversation between Stone and the local detective.

When at last he listened in, as he would have called it, Kinney was saying:

"Yes, sir, we have followed up many clues, which though promising at first, led nowhere. But—"

"I'll finish for you," said Fibsy, saucily, "but you feel sure now, you are working in the right direction and will soon be in full possession of the facts. You are not at present ready to announce your decision, but expect soon to make public some interesting disclosures."

Kinney was furious, as this was just about what he had meant to say. He gave Fibsy a withering glance, which that young hopeful received with a knowing wink.

"I'll tell you what, Mr. Kinney," he said, "you're pretty sure, aren't you, that Miss Fuller is concerned in this matter—this crime, I mean."

"I am sure of that!" Kinney exclaimed, "and if I could get hold of her—"

"I'm going to find her," McGuire said, calmly, "and then she and I will prove to you that she is utterly and entirely innocent."

"Ah, and who is the guilty person, may I ask?"

"You may ask and you may answer. I'm sure I don't know."

"Behave yourself, Terence," Stone admonished him, and seeing no chance of more fun at the expense of Detective Kinney, Fibsy wandered away.

He went in search of Tessie, with whom he had already made friends.

"Tell me something, sweetie," he said, with a cherubic smile, "tell your little Fibsy something, will you?"

"Go along with you,—you, and your foolishness," and Tessie involuntarily smiled back at the impudent chap.

"No, seriously, now. Tell me what sort of clothes and things Miss Fuller took when she went away that day."

"Why, she took no clothes at all,—no dresses or hats. I mean she took what we call an overnight bag,—only her night things, and brushes and such."

"Yes,—but I mean did she take her best night things,—as if she was going to a swell party?"

"Why—let me see. No, as I remember, she took rather her plainer things,—no boudoir cap and only a simple kimono,—no fancy negglegy."

"Yes," and the red head nodded with satisfaction. "Say, like she was going to see some friend who wasn't one of the tip-top upper crust?"

"Well, yes, you might put it so."

"And, say, Tessie,—oh, now do try! Can't you think of something she said that would give the leastest, tiniest hint of where she was going?"

"No, I can't," but urged by the earnestness of her interlocutor, Tessie thought hard.

Finally she said, "There's just one thing; in the car, on the way to the station, I caught sight of a New York Central time table in Miss Fuller's bag—the Harlem Division—"

"Oh, you duck! you daisy!" and Fibsy grabbed the girl in his arms, and made her dance a two-step while he whistled a lively tune.

"Behave yourself, you young rascal," Tessie cried, as she shook him off. "I'll not stand for such goings on!"

"You needn't," he cried, "I'm going off—way off!"

He ran away and presented himself at the door of the library, where Loft still sat at his desk.

"Mr. Loft," he said, respectfully, "may I have a talk with you?"

"Come in," Loft said, his attention arrested by something in Fibsy's tone.

"I think I may be able to locate Miss Fuller, sir," he said, a little embarrassed as he felt Loft's grave gaze fixed on his face.

"Just how?" and Loft spoke kindly.

"I'd rather not tell you," Fibsy replied. "I know that sounds queer, sir, but Mr. Stone, he knows, and he can tell you if he chooses. But it would sound to you like a wild goose chase,—and yet,—Mr. Loft,—wild geese have been caught."

Fibsy did not smile, and his look was so beseeching Loft listened with interest.

"Yes, McGuire, they have. Well, what can I do in the matter?"

"Just this, sir. Will you give me some message, which, if Miss Fuller hears it, she'll know that you want her to come back. I mean some sort of blind message,—that only she will understand,—but that she can make no mistake about."

"H'm,—I see. Well, tell her—tell her—there's a Valentine waiting for Pauline. How's that?"

"Fine! Splendid. Now, is there any other word,—any phrase that is sort of a by-word—sort of a secret between you two?"

"Why, yes, we had many of them. Tell her, for instance: 'The Portuguese are the people!' She'd understand *that* was a message from me."

"Very well, sir," Fibsy jotted the lines down in his note-book with painstaking care. "Now, will you give me five hundred dollars to spend on this thing? It's a lot of money, but I feel sure it will give you back your lady."

"You are a most extraordinary youth!" Loft said, "but I'll chance it. Here is your money. Where are you going?"

"To Springfield, Mass.," said Fibsy.

CHAPTER 16

CURRAN'S CRUELTY

PAULINE FULLER was both listless and restless. The quiet, secluded home of Mary Malden was sanctuary indeed, and Pauline ran little or no chance of being discovered there.

But now that she had had time to think matters over, she was not quite sure she had been wise in coming. She had told kind-hearted Mary her whole story, and Mary had sympathized and had coddled her and petted her, all of which was balm to Pauline's tortured heart.

Now three or four days had passed and the monotony of the place, though restful and soothing, had begun to get on her nerves.

She wondered what Val was doing. What he was thinking of her. How matters were progressing at Valhalla.

"Do you know," she said to Mary, "sometimes I feel as if I must rush right back there,—I'm so anxious about Val."

"Better stay where you are," said the practical Mary. "From what you've told me of his ideas about divorce, I should think you'd never dare see him again."

"Perhaps he'd forgive it all," said Pauline, hopefully.

"Perhaps he wouldn't," returned Mary. "No, my child, you did the most scandalous thing I ever heard of,—to pass yourself off as a girl, when you were a married and divorced woman. I wouldn't have believed it of you, Polly."

"I know it was dreadful, but oh, Mary,—I was so young, and I was urged into that marriage against my will. Almost nobody knew anything about it. I was out in California two years, you see, and the whole courtship, engagement, marriage and divorce all occurred within the first year. So, when I did come back to New York, I tried to forget it,—I told no one, not even Auntie,—she would have been so upset. And, you see, the courts gave me back my maiden name,—so I just put that whole year out of my mind,—and strove to forget it. And I did forget it, practically. I know it was wrong to deceive Val, but—he is so dear,—and he is so terribly opposed to divorce. I meant to tell him before we were married, though,—" she broke off, and bowing her head in her hands, she wept silently.

"There, there, dearie," said the kindly Mary, "never mind now, we'll think out what's best to do. But don't go back to Valhalla,—you'd—you'd be arrested for—for—you know—"

"For the murder of Hugh Curran? But I didn't kill him, Mary."

"Thank Heaven for that! Do you know, Polly, this is the first time you've said that definitely. Can I believe you, dear?"

"Oh, yes, indeed you can. No, Mary, I was in his room that night, I did take the watch, but I didn't poison him."

"Tell me about it."

"I can't, dear,—the mere thought of it all upsets me so. Just think, I hadn't thought of that man for nearly six years,—I mean, thought of him coherently. If ever a suggestion of him came in my mind I resolutely put it away from me. You know, I had no idea that Hugh Curran was Hugh Dwyer."

"You hadn't?"

"Oh, no, indeed. I had never heard from or of Hugh Dwyer since I left him at the time of the divorce—"

"Was he very dreadful to you, dear?"

"Awful! Horrible! Don't ask me about that! The divorce was granted at once,—an absolute decree and all that. Mary, *don't*!"

"No, I'll never mention it again. Go on, about this later time."

"Well, I heard them talking about this author of detective stories,—I never read them myself,—and I heard them say that Hugh Curran had been a Moving Picture actor. But it all meant nothing to me. I never connected that name with the name of Hugh Dwyer,—why should I?"

"Of course not, dearie. And then, Val invited him to the house?"

"Yes,—and it happened that when somebody asked Val what the man looked like, just out of foolishness, Val described him as quite different from the truth."

"Why did he do that?"

"No reason but as a bit of fooling. Anyway, that made me think of the coming guest as a total stranger, of course, and, Mary, when he came,—and I saw him,—I almost fainted. Truly I did. I was pouring coffee, and let the cup overflow while I struggled to keep my composure. I think I only did keep up because I knew Hugh's eye was on me, and he would be rejoiced to see me collapse."

"What a fiend he was!"

"Oh, yes, all of that. He had a diabolical way of tormenting any one, under cover of utmost friendliness. So, first of all, he asked me to walk in the garden with him,—alone. I shouldn't have gone, but anyway, Val forbade it, and Hugh subsided. Then later, he took a fiendish delight in flinging out allusions that only I could understand. Why, he even asked me straight out if I kept my bureau drawers in order,—that had been a source of disagreement between us when we lived together. He was a most untidy sort of person,—I mean about keeping things in their places. And then,—when I wouldn't seem to notice anything he said of that sort, he asked if the name 'Rosalie' meant anything to anybody present! He thought I'd betray myself then, but I didn't. Rosalie or Rosy is what he always called me because of my pink cheeks— which I always had then."

"And which you've never had since, you poor darling. Pauline, how you have suffered! Surely you've atoned for anything you have ever done."

"Oh, I hope so,—but Mary, I haven't done anything wrong—except to keep from Val the knowledge of my former marriage,—and I did that more for his sake than for my own. Truly I did."

"It was wrong, Pauline,—very wrong. But, go on, tell me the rest of your story."

"Then, he flashed his watch open once or twice, in such a way that I couldn't help seeing that my picture was in it. He used to have it there,—I don't know whether he carried it all these years or not. And,—Mary, the worst of all, was the look of admiration he gave me every chance he could get to do so, unobserved. I could have stood better his hate, his fury, his revenge, even, than those glances of admiration and apparent affection. As we said good-night, he managed to whisper to me, 'Come to my room at two o'clock.' Mary, I didn't dare disobey,—and, too, I felt I had to see him alone,—and learn what his intentions were. If he meant to expose me, I wanted it done all at once,—not by that slow torture. If I could persuade him to keep my secret, I meant to do so. Anyway my relations to Val, my hope of happiness with him, all depended on that man's attitude in the matter. So,—I went to his room—at two o'clock."

"I don't blame you, dear. You had to do it."

"Yes, I had to. And Mary, the whole trouble was that he had become infatuated with me all over again! He was engaged to another girl, but he told me he didn't love her,—and he did love me,—and he begged me to come back to him,—said I had grown more beautiful, more dear and sweet, and he wanted me. He said, if he couldn't have me,—no one else should. He said he would tell Val the whole story, and as he well knew Val's feelings about divorce, he knew—and I knew,—that would break off our engagement.

"He upbraided me fearfully for deceiving Val,—called me terrible names, and then he would change to a wheedling love-making on his own account. Finally, he threatened that unless I would promise to break with Val and remarry him, he would not only tell the whole story of our marriage, but would compromise me by saying I had come to his room that night without invitation. Oh, he was a devil incarnate. And all the time, suave and urbane as if he were proposing some casual plan. Then he would suddenly break into protestations of passion and love for me,—all of which I knew by heart, and they brought back the old days that I have tried so hard to forget. Mary,—I was ready to kill either him or myself,—and I didn't care much which."

"You didn't do either?"

"I see you can't believe me,—and I don't wonder,—now that you know what happened. No, I didn't kill him,—though I confess there was murder in my heart. And if I had had a weapon, I could have easily brought myself to do it—oh, no, I don't think I could, either. I've crime enough on my shoulders, without adding murder to it."

"No, Polly, if you didn't kill him, you've no crime to regret. Your deception of Val is wrong,—very wrong,—but not a crime. But Val knows the truth of that, now,—and Pauline, don't you suppose Val thinks you killed Curran?"

"Maybe he does,—but, Mary, how could I kill him? What with?"

"Why, with the poison,—your choice of a method, as you've told me yourself."

"But I didn't," Pauline reiterated. "I became frightened at his wild protestations of love and passion, and I simply ran out of the room. I felt sure that for all his threats he wouldn't follow me, and so, I grabbed his watch as I fled, with a half-conscious idea of destroying that picture. But when I reached my room, I was trembling so, and so faint from nervous reaction, I hid the watch and fell on the bed where I lay for hours just as I was. It was daybreak before I got up and undressed and really went to bed. Then, Mary,—then imagine next morning, learning that Hugh Dwyer was dead!"

"You were glad?"

"Glad faintly expresses it! I was freed from a dreadful danger, saved from an awful fate. I was so glad I could have sung for very joy. I daresay it was a sort of nervous hysteria, but it was all I could do to preserve a decent calm. I tried not to lie to Val. He asked me straight out if I had ever seen Hugh Curran before he came to the house. And I said 'No,' for surely I had never met Hugh Curran before. Hugh Dwyer was my persecutor. And, now, as you say, Mary, Val knows my story, and others know it. I heard enough to know they were going to send a man to Reno to learn the details of Dwyer's marriage and divorce, and the name of his wife. I knew, too, that that Detective Kinney had found the watch in my room,—with my picture in it—oh, Mary, I couldn't face Val! Now, I almost wish I had,—maybe he would have stood by me,—maybe I could have convinced him that I didn't kill Curran."

"Who do you suppose did, Pauline?"

"I can't imagine,—nor can I see how it was done. I've thought over it so much. How could any one have poisoned that man after I left his room?"

"How long after?"

"A couple of hours, I should judge. The doctors calculated that he died between four and five o'clock in the morning. I should think it a suicide, but that I know he was too eager to live to—to punish me,—or,—to marry me again. Nor can I think of any one who had any motive to kill him. I feel sure now, it must have been some intruder from outside,—maybe through the window,—though they say that was impossible. Oh, dear, I wish you'd believe, Mary, that I didn't kill him."

"I do believe it, Pauline,—at least, I'm trying to believe it. But if you had done it, I'd think you were justified,—"

"No, not justified. You may say you could understand my doing it,—as I confess I had the will to do it—oh, Mary, does that make me a murderess? Am I all bad?"

"No, no, dearie, there, there, don't cry so…. You're just a normal, true woman,—you love Val, and all these feelings toward that brute who ruined your life are only natural. How did you come to marry him, Pauline?"

"Oh, I was very young,—only seventeen, but younger even than that in my innocence and ignorance. He was a handsome, beguiling chap, and one night he made desperate love to me, and urged me to elope with him. I thought it all very romantic, and I thought I loved him,—and I went.

"We were married at once, by some clergyman friend of his, and all of the honeymoon he was angelic. But soon after, he began to be careless and worthless, and from that on, as I soon found I didn't really love him, he became cruel, brutal and unbearable. I went to stay with a friend, a nice elderly lady, and she advised me to get a divorce at once. She helped me put it through, and inside of eight months I had been wooed, wedded and divorced. Oh, but I was glad to be free again. Then when I returned to New York, a year later, I kept it a secret, to save myself the gossip that it would have caused. And when I met Val,—and when we came to love each other,—I should have told him all, but for his strange, almost insane hatred of divorce. I meant to tell him, even then, but I've put it off because I couldn't bear to hurt him. And, I've worried myself sick over the question of whether to tell him at all or not. One day I would decide to make a clean breast of it all, and then he'd say something about divorce, and I'd find myself utterly unable to open the subject. But I never should have married him without telling."

"Well, Pauline, I'm your friend, whatever happens. I'm ready to believe you didn't kill that man, but I couldn't blame anybody who thinks you did. And, I may as well say that I think if you had killed him, you'd deny it just as you have done."

Pauline smiled. She felt such a relief at having unburdened her, whole heart to her friend, that she was able to see the absurdity of Mary's attitude.

Yet was it so absurd? Could friendship go further than to pledge continued friendship even in the face of such uncertainty as was surely in Mary's mind?

Pauline appreciated this, and flung her arms round Mary while she thanked her for her goodness and love.

"And now," Mary said, with her usual good sense, "put it all out of your mind for the moment. Go and lie in the hammock and read a foolish novel or go out and pick flowers or get out some sewing,—no, don't do anything conducive to thought. Go and listen in on the radio."

"I hate those radio things," Pauline said, laughing. "To me, they're the monotonous lingo of a metal mind."

"Oh, come, now, some of it is real interesting,—and instructive, too. Go and try it, anyway."

Pauline drifted about, lounged in the hammock, picked some flowers, and honestly endeavored to put her troubles away from her for a time.

"I'm going to the village, in the Ford," Mary said, later. "Want to go?"

"No," said Pauline, promptly, "somebody might see me."

"Fiddlesticks! You can't live all your life shut up on this farm. Well, all right, but you've got to go with me tomorrow, or soon."

"Very well, we'll see," and Pauline waved a good-bye after the departing car, and returned to her listless idleness.

At last, in sheer desperation, she turned to the radio outfit, and took up the receivers.

As she had anticipated, she was bored by a soprano solo by a high-strung young girl, and an accordion obbligato by a clever young man.

She was about to disconnect, when she heard the announcement of a lecture on "European Countries Little Known." The day's subject turned out to be Portugal. Slightly interested, she listened to the lecturer's trite and ready-made phrases. And then, he said, in especially clear accents, "The Portuguese are the people!"

Pauline smiled to herself, for that was a phrase she and Val had often used, and to them it meant an appreciation of certain "Sonnets from the Portuguese," with which Elizabeth Barrett Browning charmed all lovers.

The lecture proceeded, and three times the speaker repeated the short phrase, "The Portuguese are the people."

Pauline pondered long, after the lecture was over.

Could it be a sort of an omen,—a hint from Fate that Valentine was thinking of her,—perhaps still loving her?

And then, realizing the absurdity of her own thoughts, she put it from her mind. She had no leanings toward the occult, or even toward telepathy or thought transference. And, too, as she said to herself, it wasn't Val who was doing the lecturing.

But the result of the episode was that Pauline spent many hours at the radio apparatus the next few days. She let herself be bored by the lectures on science, by the children's stories, by the far from first-class music, and by the rehash of current events. She listened even to the talk on home-making and culinary doings, hoping against hope that something would again remind her of Valentine.

At last she was rewarded. On the second day of her radio interest, there was a talk by one of New York's most celebrated detectives. Among other things he spoke of the work of the Bureau of Missing Persons. And, she could scarcely believe her ears, but she certainly heard him say, "For example, if an advertisement were worded, 'Pearline, come back and all will be forgiven,' it might not succeed in its purpose. But if it said, 'Pearline, come back, I love you,' then maybe she would come."

The lecture, though of serious intent, was in a popular style, and Pauline gasped.

For Pearline was a foolish nickname that Val used in his gayest moments. It had seemed to him a great joke to call the dignified and beautiful Pauline by the silly name.

And as she continued to listen, the lecturer referred again to the supposed advertisement and repeated the whole idea.

Pauline waited till the lecture was over and then went away to her own room to think it out.

She knew little of the way in which radio stuff was "broadcasted," but she felt almost certain that that bit in an otherwise impersonal lecture couldn't be mere chance.

If Val had wanted to send her a message, what could he have said more perfect, more poignant, than "Come back,—I love you."

How it was done, she didn't know,—but her heart claimed the message, even though her mind refused to believe it was from Valentine Loft.

Though tempted to tell Mary about it, she couldn't bring herself to do so, but she continued to haunt the radio at every number of its programmes.

"Well, for any one who scorned that thing, you've certainly become addicted to it," Mary said, as Pauline refused to leave the instrument to go for a short drive.

"I've learned to like it," Pauline said, and waved Mary to silence.

Yet only once again did she get anything from it that might have been meant for her.

It was twilight, their early supper was over, for Pauline had insisted that Mary retain her simple ways of living, and though her hostess called to her from the veranda, Pauline replied that she would come out as soon as she had heard the evening concert.

And after two or three uninteresting numbers, a fairly good baritone voice sang a ballad with a simple air, the refrain of which was: "There's a Valentine a waiting for Pauline."

No mistake this time! Pauline's eyes filled with tears and her heart beat fast as she listened to words, homely, but loving and sincere,—each stanza closing with the refrain, "There's a Valentine a waiting for Pauline."

Not Pearline this time,—but Pauline, her own name, and Valentine, her waiting lover.

Now, she knew it was intentional, now she knew it was meant for her, and she believed the references to Portuguese and to Pearline were also meant for her.

How it had been done she didn't know,—but, she assumed Valentine had somehow managed to get in on the radio programmes.

What should she do? She couldn't doubt that it was his method of trying to find her. She couldn't doubt that it was his wish that she should return to him, and that he still wanted and loved her.

She went out to the porch and told Mary Malden all about it.

"H'm," said that astute individual. "Tricky, if you ask me. And I don't believe your Val did it at all,—I believe it's the work of those smarty detectives,—they're trying to find you, and they are tricking you with that stuff. For, Valentine Loft couldn't get those things into a radio programme himself,—they won't touch anything personal. But the police could do it, of course."

Pauline was crestfallen. Suppose it should be the police, pretending to send a message from Val, so that she would by chance hear it, and divulge her hiding place!

The more she thought it over, the more it seemed that Mary must be right, and she would better not follow it up at all.

But after she went to bed that night, she lay long awake thinking. And the more she thought the more she felt she must speak to Val, let the result be what it might.

Hastily donning kimono and slippers, she went noiselessly downstairs to the telephone. She called up Long Distance, and finally succeeded in getting connection with Valhalla. The servant who answered her, went immediately to call Loft.

"Is that you, Val?" she said, timidly.

"Yes, Pauline, darling. I am coming to you. Where are you?"

Now that she had succeeded, she was panic-stricken, but his dear voice reassured her, and she whispered Mary Malden's name before the receiver fell from her trembling fingers.

CHAPTER 17

ON TO MAPLEDALE

IT was shortly before midnight that Valentine Loft received that telephone message. The rest of the household had retired, and Loft was himself preparing for bed.

"Mary Malden," he said to himself, as he hung up the receiver. "I might have guessed it! Just the place for her, too. Now, let's see—" He looked at his watch. "Just about twelve. I suppose I ought to tell Stone I'm going,—but I hate to waken him. Poor chap, he's been working hard today. Fibsy,—that's the ticket! He won't mind."

Going noiselessly through the halls, Loft tapped lightly at Fibsy's door. There was no response, but he could hear the boy's breathing.

"Sleeps like a log,—or a boy," he smiled to himself. Then he opened the door and went in.

"McGuire," he whispered, touching the lad on the shoulder.

"What's up?" and Fibsy was awake and alert in an instant. "Oh, Mr. Loft, have you got her? Have you?"

"Why, yes," and Loft was mystified at the question. "What do you know about it?"

"Why, I did it! I worked the radio people,—not the managers,—they didn't know about it,—"

"Why, you blessed little chap! Have you really put over something like that! Well, tell me about it some other time,—just now I want to leave a message with you for Mr. Stone. I'm going up to New England—"

"Oh, how are you going? When you coming back?" Fibsy sat upright in bed, his eyes shining, his tousled red hair shining, and his very face shining at the exciting news.

"I'm going in my car,—and I hope to be back tomorrow afternoon or evening."

"Lemme go with you? Oh, please, Mr. Loft, lemme go! I can be a help to you somehow, and I wanta go! Please lemme! I've earned it, haven't I?"

"Why, yes, if you brought this about, you have earned it. Come on then, can you dress quickly?"

"Exceedin' the limit!" and Fibsy was already out of bed and pulling on his stockings. "You goin' to drive yourself?"

"Yes; meet me at the garage in about five minutes. And say, McGuire, you write a note and stick it under Mr. Stone's door, will you? Tell him whatever you like."

"'Tis the same as done, sir," and Fibsy began to flourish a hairbrush.

And in less than fifteen minutes the two were tearing through the night in the general direction of the Berkshire hills.

"We needn't break any speed laws," Loft said, smiling at his own haste. "I want to get there by daybreak, but not sooner. We can't call on ladies before sunup, can we?"

"Where is she?" Fibsy asked, breathlessly.

"At Mapledale, a tiny village in a Berkshire valley. How did you work it, boy? That is, if you did work it?"

"I dunno whether it was my doin's or not." In his intense excitement Fibsy was lapsing into his careless diction, of which Stone daily endeavored to cure him.

"You see, Mr. Loft, I got around the lecturers and singers in three big broadcasting stations, chancin' that we'd hit Miss Fuller somehow. Course the management wouldn't allow it, for the simple reason that if they let us do it, they couldn't refuse anybody who wanted to send a personal message. Could they?"

"I suppose not,—go on."

"So I got hold of the performers,—private like,—and—well, I used up all your five hundred dollars. But I guess it paid."

"I guess it did,—if that's what brought this trip about."

"Don't you know?"

"No, I don't; Miss Fuller merely spoke to me,—and told me where she is staying."

"H'm,—maybe I wasn't so smart as I thought I was. Well, that's what I came along to see. That, and some few other matters. I told Mr. Stone in the note not to tell anybody where we'd gone."

"How can he, when he doesn't know himself?"

"I mean, I told him we were on track of Miss Fuller, but to keep it dark."

"I see. What sort of wireless messages did you send, McGuire?"

"Well, I worked one into a Kids' Bedtime Story, one into a Domestic Lecture,—on housekeeping and the use of Pearline,—"

"You rascal, how did you know that I have sometimes jokingly called Miss Fuller, Pearline?"

"Oh, me little chum, Her Royal Highness the Countess, told me that. Well, then I got a chap I know to write a song about the 'Valentine a waitin' for Pauline,' and oh, I did up some several more such stunts. It was one chance in five million that any of 'em would reach her ears,—oh, Mr. Loft,

I hope they did! I hope this whole trip is on account o' me! I put 'em on the Springfield Broadcasting Station, and on Schenectady and on Newark. Howsomever, if she'd a called anyway,—why I'm just as glad for you."

Loft smiled at the workings of the young mind that wanted the glory and honor if they were due him,—but if not, he was still ready to rejoice with those that did rejoice.

"You're sure she's where you're goin', ain't you, Mr. Loft?"

"I am sure, McGuire. I knew her voice, and I heard what she said. Yes, we'll find her, all right."

They sped on in silence, now and then broken by a few words, but each busy with his own thoughts.

Loft put determinedly from his mind all question of Pauline's conduct, past, present or future; he thought only of the fact that he was to see her, and soon.

At last the electric lights began to pale as the first gleams of dawn shone in the East. They were skimming through beautiful country, the Berkshire hills rose about them, the valleys became visible more and more plainly, and when the sun was fairly above the horizon, the travellers were nearing the village of Mapledale.

"It's on the outskirts, I think, or even farther out in the country—"

But farmers were up betimes, and directions were easily procured, so that Loft's swift roadster came to a halt at Miss Malden's side veranda, just as that lady herself opened her sitting-room door.

"My land!" she exclaimed, "what in the world do you want?" "Pauline," answered Loft, briefly but very truthfully.

"Why, she ain't up yet. You're Valentine Loft, I suppose?"

"Yes, and very much at your service. This is my young friend, Terence McGuire. Can you take us in and give us breakfast,—it is Miss Malden, isn't it?"

"Yes," said Mary Malden, melting before the magnetism of Loft's voice and manner. "Come right along in. Joe, he'll put your car away for you. A fine car, I should say."

"A fast car," Loft said, smiling. "Brought us up from Westchester County since midnight."

"You don't say! Well, that beats mine. Come on in. My, but Pauline will be surprised!"

"Will you call her,—waken her, if necessary. I don't feel as if I could wait—"

He broke off, smiling, and Mary Malden, after giving him a long look, said, "You're all right,—yes, I'll call her. You two can come along into this downstairs bedroom and wash up."

She showed them into the small, clean chamber, and went up to Pauline.

Good Mary Malden felt a slight misgiving as to how her guest would stand the shock of such sudden happiness, and she went softly into the room where Pauline lay. It was on the other side of the house and the car's arrival had not wakened her.

But at Mary's gentle touch she sat up quickly. "What is it, Mary? Something especial, I know, or you wouldn't wake me? Is it the telephone?"

"No, Pauline, dear,—it's—"

"I know! It's Val, himself! Oh, Mary!" and Pauline tossed aside the coverlets and sprang to the floor. "How did he get here? Oh, Mary!"

Mary Malden tried to help Pauline dress, but her fingers were slow and awkward compared to Pauline's flying gestures.

In less time than ever before, Pauline made a toilette that lacked no grace or charm because of its hasty completion.

Then she ran downstairs, and in a moment she was in the arms of Valentine Loft.

"Pauly! Pauly!" was all he could find to say, and Pauline said even less.

Miss Malden discreetly retired to the kitchen, to order extra breakfast, but Fibsy, unabashed in the presence of this unembarrassed demonstration, stood looking at the pair.

Nor did they mind at all.

"Well, Terence," Loft said, after a moment, "this is Miss Fuller. Pauline, Mr. McGuire."

"Aw, I'm just Fibsy," the boy said, abashed now that attention was drawn to himself. "But, I say, Mr. Loft, I'm glad you've got her!"

"So am I," and Loft kissed Pauline again. "Now tell us, Pauly," he said, "did you get any radio message?—young McGuire, here, will burst if he doesn't find that out soon."

"Yes, I did,—and, Val,—that's why I telephoned."

"Oh, bless the Lord!" cried Fibsy, piously. "It worked, it worked! Shades of Vidocq and Lecoq, am I the little wizard,—or ain't I?"

"You certainly are, Fibs," and Loft was as astonished and as grateful as even the boy could wish.

Mary Malden came in to hear about it, and as they sat down to her excellent breakfast they went over Fibsy's clever and successful plan in all its details.

"But," and Loft looked at Pauline reproachfully, "you ought to have called me without that."

After breakfast the pair were left alone, and then, for the first time a sudden constraint fell on them.

Pauline, all at once became aware of the wrong and injustice that she had done this man, and almost began to doubt his forgiveness.

"Don't, dear heart," he said, reading her thoughts, "don't feel that way about it. I understand,—see, I understand perfectly why you had to—yes, you just *had* to, keep your poor little secret from me. I was a brute to denounce divorce so emphatically as I did, but since I did, of course you couldn't tell me your own history. Now, forget it, darling, once and for all. It's past history; your life with Curran—Dwyer, is a sealed book,—more, a destroyed book. We need never mention it again,—though should the subject come up, it is not taboo,—we are not afraid of it! It is just a negligible matter, that's all. Now, Pauline,—did you kill Curran?"

"No, Valentine," and Pauline's gaze met his own, truthfully and fearlessly.

"I knew it, dear, of course, but I had to have your word. Then will you go back home with me and face the music?"

"Of course I will."

"But it isn't pleasant music. Many people think you did kill him,—and the reason I want you to go there, is to prove your innocence."

"Can we?"

"I'm hoping Stone can do it. He's exceedingly clever,—and I think he has a few cards up his sleeve he hasn't played yet."

"Who do you think did it, Val?"

"I haven't the least idea. I can't see any way it could have been done, nor any way anybody could have done it."

"Then we must just tell the truth, and do the best we can. I suppose everybody knows about—about me?"

"Yes, dear, everybody does. But there will be no unpleasantness that I can shield you from. Pauline,—dear, will you do this? Will you marry me before we go back?"

Pauline hesitated only an instant, then, looking deep into Loft's eyes, she put her hands in his and whispered, "Yes, I will."

"Hooray!" Loft cried, in such a gay, boyish tone that Miss Malden came running in.

"What are you two grinning at?" she asked.

"We're going to be married in a few minutes," Loft replied, kissing her in the exuberance of his happiness.

"My good land!" exclaimed the spinster, equally flustered by the news and the salute. "Where? Here?"

"Of course," Pauline said, radiant with smiles. "Help us out, won't you, Mary? Can you get a minister?"

"I can," and Fibsy's red head poked itself in at the door. "I saw a dominie's sign on a church as we came through the village. Dr. Messiter, is he the one you want, Miss Malden?"

"My gracious, I don't know! Yes, I suppose so. He's my own pastor. Yes, of course; can you drive a car, boy?"

"Yep, of course. Shall I take yours, Mr. Loft?"

"No! you young rascal, you'd break every bone in its body. Take Miss Malden's Ford-Royce!"

"And do I stop at the caterer's?" Fibsy suggested, his eyes dancing.

"Yes,—here, take Matilda along with you, she'll know what to get."

"Oh, come now, Miss Malden," Loft put in, "this isn't a wedding, you know,—just a marriage. We want to get back home by noon."

"What's your hurry?"

"The matter is serious, Miss Malden. I want to marry Pauline, of course, but I want to marry her thus quickly, so I can protect her from all sorts of troubles she is up against. Get your minister, get some ice cream,—if that's what Terence wants,—he deserves it,—but don't delay us for any fol-de-rols. Am I right, Pauline?"

"Yes, Val. It is a serious matter to us all. Shall I go and dress?"

"Yes, dear, run along."

Loft's voice was infinitely gentle, and Pauline's eyes filled with tears as she went to dress for her second wedding ceremony.

Mary came to help her and it was in silence that they chose one of the few simple frocks Pauline had obtained during her stay with her friend. There was a white Canton crêpe which they agreed upon, and in less than half an hour, the bride was ready, and almost at the same moment Fibsy arrived with the clergyman, and a consignment from the confectioner's.

And then in the presence only of Mary Malden and Terence McGuire the pair were united and the benediction pronounced on their bowed heads.

The feast was done justice to by Fibsy and the minister, but the other members of the wedding party could not partake.

Pauline was nervous, but Loft was strong and firm enough for both of them.

"I can conquer anything now," he said exultantly, "since I have you for my very own," and cutting short the loving farewells between his wife and her dear friend, he tucked her into the car beside him, leaving the small rear seat for Fibsy.

Off they went, the cook Matilda appearing from the kitchen to throw some rice after them, and Miss Malden and the clergyman sat down to talk it over.

Meanwhile Loft's car flew back over the road to Valhalla. They did not go so fast but that they could enjoy the delightful ride and the still greater delight of each other's company. And Fibsy, like a veritable God of the Machine, sat up behind and blessed his lucky star that he had done something that would please F. Stone.

As they drove up to the house at last, Fibsy, jumping out of the car, was caught by Stone, who carried him off for a quick confab.

"Never mind, McGuire," Stone said, as the boy began a tale of the radio, "it was fine,—but now you're to fly to New York like a bandersnatch. There's a car waiting to take you,—go first to Hugh Curran's rooms at the hotel, here's the address, on this paper, and get from his shelves the book noted here. Then hurry around to the auction rooms,—see, the address, and bid up on this item marked in this catalogue."

"Yes, sir," and Fibsy choked back his disappointment at not telling of his triumph, while he listened carefully to Stone's directions.

"Don't bid yourself, but get some attendant there to bid for you. If you can't get the item for two hundred dollars, give it up, but go as high as that. Here's the money. Keep yourself out of sight, but notice who is bidding against you, and if it's some agent, find out, adroitly, who is his principal. Got it all?"

"Yes, sir,—Good-by. Back here?"

"Yes, as soon as possible. Keep the Loft car and come back in it. The chauffeur is at your orders. Don't muff anything, McGuire, much depends on you."

Fibsy touched his cap, and ran. He knew when Stone called him McGuire, it was because he was putting real responsibilities on him, and he was more than willing to do his best.

Once in the car, and the chauffeur speeding toward the city, Fibsy had opportunity to look over the memoranda Stone had given him, and which was clear though concise. The matter mastered, he gave himself up to the happy reflections on his good work with the radio; and on the loveliness of the lady for whom he had done it, even before he had seen her at all. He greatly admired Loft, and now, more than ever, since he had seen him rush a wedding through in less than an hour!

"Going some!" Fibsy decided, and then he curled up for a nap *en route*.

In New York he did all Stone had instructed him. He went to the hotel, got the desired book,—a queer looking old thing he thought it, too, though in a most new, shiny and elaborate case, and then he went to the auction rooms.

Fibsy had never seen a book auction before, but he was quick to apprehend conditions, and soon found an agent to bid for him. The item he was after would not be put up for half an hour or so, and Fibsy, remembering Stone's caution to keep out of sight, found a seat behind some long window draperies.

However, he saw no one he knew, except Bob Baldwin, who he supposed went to all book auctions.

"Funny business, dealing in old ragged books," he thought, but as he watched the proceedings he soon learned that wiser heads than his set great value on the antique volumes.

At last the item he was interested in went up at sale.

To his surprise it was only one page of a book! What in the world could any one want of one page! But the bidding was brisk, and soon the hundred-dollar mark was passed.

Fibsy's agent kept on, and as the bids became higher, more bidders dropped out. At last the agent kept on against one other only, and finally as two hundred was overbid, Fibsy's agent ceased, and the page went to the other bidder.

"Who's it gone to?" Fibsy asked of his man, as he returned the money Fibsy had advanced.

"To Mr. Baldwin,—he's a swell dealer,—doesn't even call himself a dealer,—a commission buyer. He would have gone on forever, I guess. Probably had an unlimited bid for somebody."

"Prob'ly," agreed Fibsy, for Stone had told him not to chatter.

Into the car and home to the Loft place the boy went next, taking care not to be seen by Baldwin, who left the auction room just ahead of him.

On the way home, Fibsy mused over the strange vagaries of this game of book collecting, and determined to study up the matter. He didn't like to be so utterly ignorant of anything that might mean so much.

He went at once to Stone with his report and received that gentleman's unstinted praises for the work in New York, and also for the ingenious radio stunt he had pulled off.

Fibsy blushed with pleasure at receiving the highest compliments Fleming Stone had ever yet paid him.

"Aw, shucks," he said, greatly embarrassed, "it wasn't anything of a trick. I just happened to pull it off. Now, F. Stone, where do we stand?"

Stone looked grave.

"The case is about finished," he said slowly. "I'm sorry at the results, but we must take what comes."

"You know who killed Mr. Curran?"

"Yes, Fibs."

"You know how and why?"

"Yes."

"When do I get it?"

"After dinner tonight, in the library, I shall have to tell all."

"I'll be there," said Terence McGuire.

CHAPTER 18

THE TRUTH AT LAST

DINNER at Valhalla that night partook of the nature of a wedding feast.

Pauline, now that there was no longer any secret about her past, blossomed into a happy bride, and except for the cloud of tragedy that still hung over the household, all was serene and almost jubilant.

Loft was unable to contain his joy, and almost forgot the Curran affair in his new-found happiness.

But not every one was so sure of Pauline's innocence as was her new-made husband and her intimate friends.

In fact, Kinney had sent a message that he must have an interview with her that evening, and Stone, to whom the matter was referred, sent back a message for Kinney to come to the house at nine o'clock.

Hetty Dwyer was frantic.

Knowing all she now knew, she was positive Pauline had killed her brother and even went so far as to hint that it was because the divorce was not absolute, and that he was an obstacle in the way of Pauline's marriage to Loft.

"What have you done, Mr. Stone?" she burst out during the dinner hour. "What have you accomplished? Have you established Miss Fuller's innocence,—or Mr. Loft's? For my part I could easily believe that he killed my brother on Miss Fuller's behalf! So far as I can see, you have sat around here for four or five days and have done nothing—nothing at all! You have refused to cooperate with the police, yet you have done nothing by yourself to solve the mystery. You accept the story Miss Fuller tells, you look no further, but, influenced by her feminine charm, you believe her unsupported word. Myself, I know her of old,—I know—"

"There, there, Miss Dwyer," Stone said, gently, "don't fling questions at me so rapidly. Nobody could answer that rapid-fire list,—I doubt if you remember them yourself. And, too, I submit that I have made some progress in this matter. But I don't think the subject a good one for dinner-table conversation, and I will ask you to wait until we can all adjourn to the library. Then I have a few statements to make."

"I'm glad to hear that," the Countess exclaimed. "I confess that I'm growing impatient. It's delightful to have Pauline and Val married, but I shall feel more quiet in my mind when this other matter is settled. As a matter of fact, I want to get away, but I won't go, until I learn the results of Mr. Stone's investigation of this case."

"We want to go, too," Anna said; "and Ned won't stir a step until the whole thing is settled."

"I can't desert the ship," Knox put in. "Val and Angel and Roly and I are a sort of committee to look into this horrid affair, and I'm sure not one of us will leave until we know the truth. I admit we have none of us done much to help the investigation, but that isn't because we haven't tried."

"And, too, it isn't necessary for us to do anything now that Mr. Stone is on the job," said Angel, looking at the detective. "But I shall be glad to get away soon, for the book auction sales are beginning and I've some special orders on hand."

"You can run back and forth in the cars, whenever you like, Bob," Loft said. "Just give your own orders."

"Thank you, Val, but I ought to be back in town soon."

"As far as the discovery of the facts regarding the death of Mr. Curran is concerned, I can tell you that this evening," Stone said, as Pauline rose from the table.

She had taken her place as mistress of Valhalla easily and naturally. Secure in her own knowledge of her innocence, sure that none of her real friends suspected her, she also felt confidence that Fleming Stone would prove her case to the local police,—and then, she hoped, she and Loft could go away for a honeymoon.

But a little later, when the party had gathered in the library, and when Detective Kinney arrived, Pauline saw from his unfriendly glances that the local police still deemed her guilty,—or, at least, implicated in the tragic death of Hugh Curran.

"To begin with," Stone said, "you remember that there was a discussion as to the preferable method of killing a man."

"Oh, don't rake that up again," Ned Knox almost groaned. "I'm positive that none of us who took part in that fool discussion ever carried out any such a plan."

"You may be sure of that,—but I'm not," Stone said, and he looked at Knox so earnestly, that Roly Mears concluded at once that Ned was the murderer after all!

"But, leaving that for the moment," Stone went on, "I will tell you first, what I discovered from an examination of Mr. Curran's body. Although the doctors made a careful autopsy, they didn't chance to discover what I found,—by looking for it. That is a small puncture in the jaw of the dead man, through which, there can be no doubt, the poison was introduced into his system."

"The hypodermic needle!" cried Roly Mears, quickly.

"I haven't said so," Stone returned, "but I do say that 'the needle' figured prominently among the clues I have worked from."

"What needle?" Angel asked, interestedly.

"Oh, an old needle——" Stone began, "that——"

"Oh," Roly exclaimed, "an old rusty needle! Blood poisoning!"

"Suppose you let Mr. Stone do the talking," Kinney growled out; "we are more interested in his recital, Mr. Mears, than in your comments."

Before Roly could resent this speech, Stone resumed.

"Without further delay," he said, "I will tell you what I at first assumed. If I wrongly suspected an innocent man, wait, at least, until you hear the whole story."

"Miss Fuller,—I beg your pardon,—Mrs. Loft, will you answer a few questions?"

"Certainly," said Pauline, a little agitated, but reassured by Loft's clasp of her hand.

"Then you are willing to state that you visited Mr. Curran,—whom you knew as Mr. Dwyer, in his room that night?"

"I did."

"As late as two o'clock, or after?"

"Yes."

"For what purpose?"

"To ask him to stop persecuting me, and to obtain from him my picture which he had in his watch-case."

"And his attitude?"

Pauline hesitated, then said, bravely, "He was, he stated, still fond of me, and asked me to remarry him. When I refused, he became sarcastic and even brutally rude. I knew from something he had said, that he had some letters of mine with him,—I knew that he probably had hidden them in a drawer beneath his handkerchiefs,—for—I knew his ways. I found the letters, and I took them, also I took his watch, which then lay on the table between us, and I ran away to my own room."

"Leaving Mr. Curran alive and well?"

"Perfectly so. He was laughing at my discomfiture as I closed the door behind me. He chose to treat the whole matter lightly,—though to me it was even then a tragedy."

"Yes; now, think carefully, Mrs. Loft. Did you chance to see on the table, or anywhere, a toothpick sealed in a printed paper?"

"Yes, there was one there,—a Country Club one. I paid no attention to it, but I do remember that it was there. Why?"

"I will tell you in a moment. Remember it well,—it may prove to be an alibi. However, you have an alibi aside from that. The doctors are agreed that Mr. Curran died not earlier than four o'clock in the morning. Therefore, he was alive at least an hour and a half after your departure from his room. Mr. Meredith fixed that time at two-thirty, and you say that yourself. Now, if Mr. Curran was killed by the poison at four o'clock, who could have done it? Also, how did the murderer make his exit?"

"May I call your attention to the fact, Mr. Stone," said Kinney, ponderously, "that those are the questions that have confronted us from the beginning."

"Yes, but I have learned the answers to them, Mr. Kinney."

"Indeed,—and how did the murderer get in?"

"Mr. Curran let him in."

"And how did he leave the room?"

"Mr. Curran let him out."

"You are pleased to be mysterious."

"Not at all. The murderer did not do his killing while he was in the room."

"Then Mr. Curran killed himself?"

"No, I do not put it that way. But I will tell you my discovery. The puncture in Mr. Curran's jaw, which I discovered, is inside the mouth, and against a molar tooth. Can you wonder, that I deduced a poisoned toothpick? At any rate I did conclude that the instrument of death, for I could find no other. I pictured Mr. Curran, after Miss Fuller's departure, sitting down to think matters over, perhaps eating a few of the nuts of which he was fond, and then, naturally, using the toothpick,—which, let us say, had been previously dipped in hydrocyanic acid."

"Could such a case be possible?" asked Kinney.

"Yes," Stone replied, "I have consulted with expert chemists who assure me it is entirely possible."

"You're making it sound like my work," Angel said, with a rueful glance at Stone. "But I plead not guilty."

"And wisely," Stone returned. "Indeed, the first thing I did after these discoveries was to examine the quill toothpick which I found in the wastebasket. It was absolutely free from any trace of poison."

"Then who did it?" Bob asked, his handsome face eagerly inquisitive.

"That's what I wondered," Stone said; "for I was so sure I had struck the right trail. Of course, I knew that Mr. Baldwin had given Curran that Club toothpick, and it seemed a clever deduction. But that clue failed. So then I began to hunt a motive. And the motive I found."

"The motive!" cried Miss Dwyer; "then you can tell who killed my brother. Tell us quickly, Mr. Stone."

"As quickly as possible. But the truth is so strange, the evidence so slight, the clues so hazy that though I am convinced myself, I cannot convince you unless you listen attentively and follow closely my arguments. I am sure, now, that the man who killed Mr. Curran was actuated by some circumstance connected with Mr. Curran's collection of books."

"That interests me," Angel said; "I've rather suspected that all along."

"Yes," Stone proceeded. "Now, the night of his death, Mr. Curran was deeply interested in some items in certain catalogues."

"He was," Angel nodded. "He discussed them with me."

"One catalogue in particular, Mr. Curran possessed, was not found in his room, afterward."

"How do you know?" Kinney asked.

"Because it was the catalogue that contained 'The Needle.'"

"'The Needle!'" Knox cried; "was that a book, then?"

"Yes; any great collector would know at once, that it means a very old and rare book, called 'Gammer Gurton's Needle'—a volume dated 1575."

"My brother had that book in his library," said Miss Dwyer, proudly. "I remember it well."

"So does Mr. Baldwin, no doubt," Stone said; "in fact, Mr. Baldwin bought it for him."

"I did," said Angel, "and I had a high old time to find a copy."

"Yes; now, in this catalogue I speak of there was not a copy of this book for sale, but there was a single page of it. As some of you may not know, book collectors pay good prices for even one leaf of a very rare book."

Fibsy sat on the edge of his chair, enthralled by the conversation. Well he knew, after his afternoon's experience, how collectors bid up on the single leaf of a rare book!

"Well," Stone proceeded, "as is generally known, there are unscrupulous book dealers as well as dealers in other wares. Now, a favorite scheme of theirs is to utilize in various ways these single leaves."

"Aside from selling them as fragments?" Loft inquired.

"Oh, yes. They are really ingenious about it. Take this 'Gammer Gurton's Needle,' for instance. It was published in London by Thomas Colwell, in 1575. Now, you can easily see, that the title page of such a book would be its chief requisite. The title page missing, the volume would be worth little in comparison with a perfect copy. So, the clever book dealer, substitutes another title page, and so produces what is apparently a complete copy."

"Where does he get the other title page?" asked Baldwin, his supercilious air denoting his superior knowledge of these matters.

"That's the ingenious part of it. He photographs the real one."

"I've heard of it," Bob said, "but I doubt if it can be done successfully. I know about these things, you see."

"It might not be done in a manner to deceive you, Mr. Baldwin, or any one who is a real connoisseur,—but it could easily fool the average reader,—even the average collector."

"My brother's copy is perfect," Miss Dwyer informed them. "I have heard him say so,—and it has been pronounced upon by experts."

"Doubtless," agreed Stone. "Yet, here is what happened. Mr. Curran had a catalogue of an auction sale, that listed a page of this old book. Whereupon, he went to his own copy and on examination found that several pages of his book had been extracted and photographed pages had been put in their places. This must have been done, Miss Dwyer, since the expert you spoke of examined the book.

"However, it had been done, and naturally, Mr. Curran was greatly astounded and that was the matter of 'The Needle' he was discussing with Mr. Baldwin."

"Yes," and Bob nodded his head, gravely. "I hoped to keep the matter quiet, until I could discover who did it. But since you know of it, I will ask you to consider it confidential. I secured one of the missing pages at a sale this afternoon,—and I hope to get the others. I told Mr. Curran I hoped to do this, and he was greatly pleased."

"Yes," Stone said; "now, you can all see, why I suspect that some one implicated in this theft is the man who put Mr. Curran out of the way. And, returning for a moment, to the matter of the toothpick, may I inquire if any one noticed a toothpick on the floor the morning the body was found."

"Yes, there was one," Knox said, thinking back. "Don't you remember, Angel, you found it on the floor—"

"And threw it in the waste-basket," supplemented Roly.

"Threw another one in!" cried Stone, triumphantly. "Mr. Baldwin is the clever criminal, he is the ingenious book thief,—it was he who provided the poisoned toothpick, and after it had done its work, he adroitly substituted a clean one for the other and placed it in Curran's waste-basket."

"Pretty work, Mr. Stone," Baldwin said, "but not very convincing. I can see how you can perhaps think that is all so, but I defy you to prove it."

"Proof isn't necessary, for you are going to confess," Stone said, coolly. "However, I will say, that here is the paper that contained the toothpick in question. A mere glance will show you all that it has been unsealed and sealed up again. This, of course, after the poisoned quill was put into it.

"Also, I have the book of Mr. Curran's that shows not only the photographed page in the middle of the book, but also photographed title page and the three back pages. You see, Mr. Baldwin borrowed this book from Mr. Curran a few months ago. He photographed the pages, and put them in the Curran copy, using the real ones to complete a deficient copy that he had been able to buy for a small price. This now perfect copy, he sold for twenty thousand dollars. The sale is on record."

"The jig is up!" Angel Baldwin said, but his face paled. Clearly his jaunty air was hard to retain. "How did you catch on, Mr. Stone?"

"Curran revealed it himself. He knew of your dishonesty. He said, you all remember, 'Mr. S.', and asked if that meant anything to anybody. It showed Mr. Baldwin that Curran knew all, and meant to follow it up."

"What had Mr. S. to do with the book?" Knox inquired.

"The title page of that old volume reads, 'Gammer Gurton's Needle, a right, pithy comedy, by Mr. S.' So, Curran's quick wit chose that way of revealing his knowledge of the theft of the pages."

"That's right," Bob said, "it's all true. The man was ingenious, and so was I. You see, he knew not only of the 'Needle' pages, but some few other similar bits of work I've put over. It doesn't hurt the collectors. If they don't know it,—and they rarely do, the books are just as good for them. And Curran brought it on himself. He threatened to expose me, wouldn't listen to my plea to hush it up if I made good to him. So,—when he wanted a toothpick,— I conjured up that scheme,—and it worked. Then I thought if I substituted a clean toothpick that next morning, it would all blow over. Of course, I should have confessed if Pauly had not been cleared. But after she was free from suspicion I thought I could brazen it out. But F. Stone is too many for me. Well, life's a gamble, and I've lost."

And then, though Stone was alertly watching for that very thing, Bob popped something into his mouth and swallowed it.

"I feared it," Stone said, springing to his side. "I watched him—but he fooled me. Perhaps it's just as well."

Perhaps it was. No one wanted to see poor old Angel stand trial whatever the outcome might have been. And there was hope for nothing but the extreme penalty.

"Who'd ever think it of Bob?" Knox exclaimed, as, the women having been put out of the room, the men clustered round the still figure.

"Yet, in a way, it was like him," Loft said, musingly. "He always wanted something for nothing,—to get money without doing work. And he thought himself so secure in this nefarious business of his, that to find Curran ready to expose him was more than he could stand. And his quick, clever brain seized on that toothpick idea at once. Of course, he had the poison stuff in his photographic outfit."

"You get out of here, Valentine," Knox said; "we'll look after all the necessary details. You go and pick up Pauline and I'll call your car, and you two fly down to New York and begin your honeymoon. Skittle, now!"

Loft hesitated a moment, but the thought of Pauline decided him. "I will, Ned, you're a brick," and Loft went off at once.

"Come, Pauly," he said, as he returned to her in the drawing room, "we're going to hook jack! Get your wraps."

"I believe I promised to obey," said Pauline, smiling through tears. "Will you look after the house, Countess?"

"Yes, of course," and getting the drift of things, the Countess and Anna hurried off with Pauline to throw some things in a suitcase for her.

And in less than a half hour the bride and groom started on their wedding journey, the rest of the household went to their rooms and Detective Kinney took charge of all that was left of the gay, careless, and irresponsible Angel Bob Baldwin, while he mused on the cleverness of the great detective who had deduced the truth from the "feathers left around."

www.ingramcontent.com/pod-product-compliance
Lightning Source LLC
Chambersburg PA
CBHW011447170626
46816CB00008B/2563